ANISHA
ACCIDENTAL DETECTIVE

SCHOOL'S
CANCELLED

SERENA PATEL
Illustrated by Emma McCann

USBORNE

CHAPTER 1

STRESSED OUT!

I think Thursdays are a funny kind of day. It's not the weekend yet, which is okay with me because weekends mean family time. Family time usually means a lot of noise and drama in our house. Don't get me wrong, I do love my family, but they're also a bit bonkers and they get themselves into trouble **A LOT**. Anyway, this Thursday is kind of a special and exciting day at school because of the **BIG ANNOUNCEMENT**!

You see, there's a science fair next week. And not just any science fair either. It's the National Schools Science Fair and whoever has the best experiment wins an amazing prize. Actually, not just amazing, it's an **intergalactic** prize – a trip to the **national**

space centre! And the winner gets to meet a real-life astronaut! **How cool is that?**

Everyone in my year is so excited, even the kids who don't normally like science. Each school can only enter two teams and today our science teacher, Miss Bunsen, is going to announce who our two teams are. She's been watching us working on our projects for the last four weeks and it's been making my tummy go all weird, because I want our team to be one of the chosen ones **SO BAD**!

Mostly I quite like school, apart from some of the other kids. When I say other kids, I actually mean the **evil twins** Mindy and Manny, my cousins (only by marriage – their dad, Uncle Tony, married my mum's sister, Aunty Bindi). And yes, I meant it when I said they're **EVIL**. They used to go to a boarding school, but Uncle Tony decided it would be better for them to be close to home, where he can keep an eye on them. It's weird, but since they've been at my school they seem to be staying out of trouble. I keep an eye on them though, as they are not to be trusted.

If that wasn't enough to deal with, I also have an arch-enemy, Beena Bhatt – she's the worst. She thinks I'm **her** arch-enemy but I'm really not. I might have **ACCIDENTALLY** knocked her over once but that doesn't mean we have to forever be arch-enemies! I have tried to tell her that but she won't listen, so now I just try to stay out of her way. It's not easy. I'd ask to be homeschooled, but that would probably be worse!

Me
+
Mum as my teacher
=
Some sort of meditating on my head and drinking green tea (bleurgh!)

On the other hand...

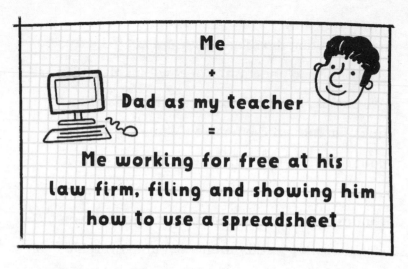

Me

+

Dad as my teacher

=

Me working for free at his law firm, filing and showing him how to use a spreadsheet

But then what about...

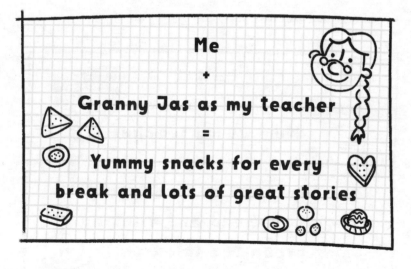

Me

+

Granny Jas as my teacher

=

Yummy snacks for every break and lots of great stories

I smile to myself, thinking about how fun it would

be to read my books all day while Granny cooked up

8

a mountain of treats. She's making parathas* this morning, which are **my favourite**. The delicious smell of a big pile of steaming fried spicy flatbreads is wafting through the house.

Dad already left at 8.14 a.m., which is exactly fourteen minutes later than he should have done. He blustered out of the door **in a whirlwind** of jangling keys, briefcase and files under his arm and a half-eaten piece of toast dangling between his teeth. I don't think I've ever seen him sit down for breakfast. Mum's gone off to the local gym to run her early morning meditation class. I'm in a rush too, because I woke up late. I was up reading by torchlight till the middle of the night, so I slept through my alarm this morning. It was Dad's **morning bathroom noises** that finally woke me. I once saw a documentary about camels and weirdly that's what my dad sounds like – gargling and gurgling every morning. For once I was glad that he's so loud!

☆☆⭐☆ ⭐ ☆☆☆⭐ ⭐☆☆ ⭐ ☆ ⭐☆⭐ ⭐ ☆ ⭐ ☆ ☆☆⭐☆ ⭐ ⭐☆☆⭐

* Parathas are just the best. They are spicy flatbreads which Granny cooks on her iron tawa pan. I love to watch her making them and the smell is amazing!

I grab a paratha from the plate Granny's piling them onto and stuff it in my mouth too fast. "**Hot, hot, hot!**" I gasp, as Granny passes me a glass of water without even turning around.

"You kids, always in a rush. Take your time, silly," she gently scolds.

"But I **am** in a rush, I'm gonna be late," I moan.

"You shouldn't stay up till who knows what time then!" Granny smiles. "You think I don't see your torchlight shining under the bedroom door as I go to my room at night? When will you learn, Granny sees everything!"

"In my defence, I was reading a maths book!" I protest. "We always have a test on Thursdays. It's my second favourite subject! Well, it used to be."

"Used to be?" Granny studies my face. "Has something happened, beta?"

"No...I mean...well, it's just I usually know the answer when the teacher asks a question and..."

"And that's a bad thing these days, is it? Don't be

shy, beta. You should never be afraid to show your talents. You are **clever**. If the teacher asks you a question, go ahead and answer."

"You don't understand," I sigh.

Granny waves her rolling pin in my direction. "Granny understands everything."

"I just think sometimes it's easier to try and blend in, be part of the crowd. Not everyone in my school thinks being clever is cool."

"**Humph**," Granny snorts. "Anni, what are you talking about? Why would you want to hide your light? You must stand out, stand up, be proud!" She puffs out her chest.

"Do you think we would be here if our ancestors had just sat there idly letting everyone else speak up for them? **No, of course not!**"

I don't really know why Granny talks about people who lived long ago when things are so different now. I couldn't be any less like my brave ancestors if I tried – speaking up isn't really my thing.

"It's not that easy these days, Granny. If you're too clever, then some of the other kids make fun of you for being a nerd. I never used to care in Year Four or even Year Five, but things seem different in Year Six. There are still lots of kids who want to study and do well, but the teacher always uses my work as an example and it's embarrassing. It's just not good to be too clever."

"**Too** clever? **Too** clever? What is that? You can never be too clever, beta. Your brain is your **super power**, it's the thing that makes you special. Only you think like you!"

"Well, I wish someone would tell certain kids in my school that being clever is super."

"I will tell them! Shall I come to school with you now? I will put on my chappals* and march down to that school and I will tell them!"

"No, no, it's fine, Granny – anyway, grown-ups aren't allowed into school and I'd, erm, better go!" I make a move towards the front door before Granny can put her chappals or anything else on and follow me.

She shouts after me, "Put your hood up, it's cold out there! That nice weatherman, Gopal Singh – you know, the handsome one? – he said we might get some rain later. And don't forget, Bindi will be round after school, she wants your help with the party. I don't know, all this fuss, completely unnecessary! In my day we sang 'Happy Birthday', we blew out the candles,

---

* Granny's chappals are her sandals. Granny doesn't wear any other type of shoe – even in winter! She just puts a pair of woolly socks on and slips her trusty Scholl chappals on over the top.

and we ate some mithai,* job done. Bindi wants fireworks and flowers and too much faffing, if you ask me."

Next weekend it's Granny's big birthday. She's going to be seventy-five – practically ancient. (But I'd never say that to her, as she'd definitely take her chappal off and throw it at me!) Dad said we should have a family gathering in honour of Granny. It was meant to be just a quiet dinner, but then Bindi got involved – my **very** melodramatic Aunty Bindi. So now it's the **Extremely Enormous Birthday Party** and suddenly there's a completely **over-the-top** three-tier cake, fantastic fireworks, immense entertainment, about a hundred guests, a ton of fabulous food and of course a massive marquee. I've been hiding from Bindi all week. She wants me to be her party-planning assistant. I mean, come on, do I

* Mithai is the yummiest Indian sweet treat and it comes in all colours and shapes.

sound like I want to be a party planner to you?!

Anyway, the big National Schools Science Fair is exactly one week from today, did I say that already? I'm in a team with Milo, of course, and our new friend Govi – he transferred from another school four weeks ago and he's really shy. We've been working on this **amazing** experiment together. It's top secret though, so I can't tell you what it is yet. And no, before you say it, that doesn't mean we haven't figured out how to do it. Well, it might need a few tweaks... The thing is, between dodging Aunty Bindi and worrying about our entry for the fair, I have been **SO STRESSED OUT**!

I try to think calming thoughts on the way to pick up Milo from his house. When I get there, Milo is standing outside, happily chatting to his pocket. He got a **pet rat** called Ralph last week.

"Milo, you can't bring Ralph to school!" I warn.

Milo grins at me. "Why not? **What could go wrong**?"

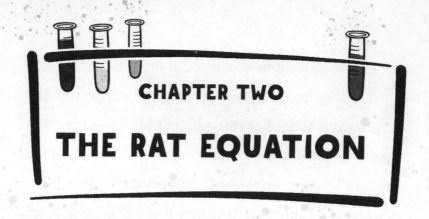

CHAPTER TWO

THE RAT EQUATION

Even though I think Thursdays are funny I actually like them quite a lot, because instead of going to our normal classroom, we head to the new lab for science, which is obviously my other absolute best lesson (as well as maths). Our school got the new science lab last year and only Year Six kids are allowed to use it. It has high benches with swivel stools and loads of fancy equipment, which we're not allowed to use unsupervised. We've been **forbidden** from any sort of fire or flammable materials until all the parents sign a form – I think our head teacher Mr Graft might be a bit worried about the school **burning down**. Anyway, everyone's always really excited for science, because it's the only lesson we have away from our normal classroom apart from PE.

"Right, children, settle down and listen up, please." Miss Bunsen, the lead teacher for science in our school, calls out the register as we pile into the lab, stools scraping on the shiny wooden floor and bags bashing against the metal table legs. I always sit with Milo and Govi. Poor Govi has really bad eyesight and as a result he has to wear the thickest glasses I've ever seen. I know some glasses are nice and trendy, but these are like **magnifying glasses**. I feel so bad for him, because the mean kids call him **Goggles** and make fun of the badges he wears on his sweater too. I like them, but cool kids like Beena think **Geology Rocks** on a badge is nerdy.

Anyway, I told him to ignore the teasing and just hang out with us. And every bit of spare time we have had recently has been spent planning, making, sticking, painting or testing for our experiment. It's going to be **AWESOME**.

"So, class, who can guess what we'll be working on today?" Miss Bunsen asks, placing the register on the desk in front of her and smiling at us expectantly.

"A clinical trial to cure geekiness, and the test subjects are on Anisha's table," snorts Beena. A few kids snigger.

"What was that, Beena dear? Speak up, it's very difficult to hear you from here." Miss Bunsen is slightly hard of hearing. I heard it's because she used to work for **NASA** and once stood too close to a rocket launch. I'm not sure if that's true.

"I said, we're here to learn of course!" Beena smiles sweetly.

Miss Bunsen eyes her suspiciously and continues, "Yes, well. As you know, the National Schools Science Fair is **next week** and we are lucky enough to be hosting it this year. I know some of you are just dying to find out who I have picked from your year to represent our school!" She pauses.

I nudge Milo, who's checking the rat is okay in his pocket – this is it. I can barely sit on my stool straight. I glance at Govi, but he's staring off towards another table. I follow his gaze and find Mindy – **evil twin number one** – glaring at me. Suddenly Miss Bunsen's voice snaps my gaze back to the front of the room.

"You have all worked very hard over the past few weeks and I've been so impressed by your ideas and enthusiasm. Unfortunately, I can only select two projects and I have picked the pupils who I think have shown the most commitment and dedication. Without further ado, the projects I have picked to represent us at the National Schools Science Fair are…"

Somebody starts a **drum roll** with their feet and the rest of the class join in.

"Adil Ansa and his ant army," Miss Bunsen announces.

Adil, our top science rival, jumps up from his stool and punches the air. **"YESSSS!"**

"And the second project representing our school is… **Anisha, Govi and Milo with their volcano demonstration.**"

Adil stops jumping up and down and shouts, **"WHAT!?"**

Milo and I ignore him and high-five each other,

except we kind
of miss. Govi
messes with
the edge of
his glasses
and smiles
nervously, but he
seems distracted. I
guess he doesn't like

being the centre of attention. But can you believe it?
We did it! We're going to be representing
the school in the science fair!

We spend the next hour imagining what it would
be like to go to the space centre and all the cool stuff
they might have there. No one gets very much work
done and Miss Bunsen is just as **excited** as us! By
the end of science, Milo and I are so fired up about
the competition and winning the trip that we decide
to come back after school later and continue working
on our entry. Miss Bunsen agrees to call our parents

to check it's okay and reassures them she'll be here to supervise. I hear the twins and Beena **tittering** as they walk out of the lesson – probably laughing at us for wanting to stay back and do extra work after school. I try to ignore them. I'm so excited about the science fair, and maybe Granny's right that I should be proud of the things I'm good at. I still don't say anything to them though. I always think of the right thing to say later on when they're not even in front of me any more. I hate that.

"You know, you children could take a leaf out of their book," Miss Bunsen calls after them. "Beena, I'm sure you could benefit from some extra study time!"

"Oh, well I'd love to, obviously." Beena smiles her sickly smile. "But Daddy insisted that I'm home on time today as we're going to a fancy restaurant for dinner. **Dear Daddykins** does like to treat me. He's sending the car for me at 3.20 p.m. on the dot." She swings her bag over her shoulder and sashays off down the corridor. Beena, like the twins, has her own driver. I don't think she's ever been on a bus or walked anywhere further than a few metres in her life.

"We've got the dentist," adds Mindy before Miss Bunsen can even ask her about staying back to do extra work.

"We have?" moans Manny. "No one told me!"

"That's because you're always such a baby about it." Mindy laughs as they walk out of class.

Last to leave before us is Adil Ansa. Adil is in the top groups for everything and is really competitive and a bit of a **know-it-all**. If you say you're going to be doing something, he's probably already done it. If you say you're feeling ill, then he's definitely feeling **worse**. And if you give an answer in class, then he'll have a better, more detailed one or a reason why your answer is wrong. So it's no surprise when he comes up to us, **scowling**.

"Just so you know," he says, "there is only

going to be **one** winner at the science fair and that is going to be **me**."

"We'll see," I reply, because that's all I can think of to say. Thankfully Adil huffs and walks off.

"How did I make so many enemies?" I sigh.

"I think that's your special talent," jokes Milo as we head out of the lab and back to our classroom for the next lesson: maths.

We walk down the hallway and file in behind some other kids. As usual, Pete Drum, one of the **loud** and **annoying** kids in our class, is being **loud** and **annoying** at the front of the room, doing bad impressions of being a teacher. **Ralph the rat** pokes his nose out of Milo's pocket, probably trying to see what all the noise is about, and Milo hurriedly tucks him back down and whispers to him to stay

put. Better hope no one
sees Ralph or there will
be **mayhem**. I can just
imagine our teacher and
all the kids freaking out.

I spot the twins straight away,
sitting in their seats at the front of the classroom.
They used to like sitting at the back, but the teacher
moved them to keep an eye on them. Manny is
already slouched in his chair, chewing gum and
playing some sort of game on his phone. We're not
supposed to have phones in school but some kids
think they don't have to follow the rules. Uncle Tony
insisted on Mindy and Manny having mobile phones
so he can keep track of them. He runs a phone shop
so they get the latest ones. I, on the other hand, am
not allowed one till I'm in senior school, which is not
till next year.

Mindy is scribbling furiously in her notebook –
she takes that thing with her everywhere. She's

probably coming up with new ways to make my life a misery. Next to Mindy and Manny is Beena Bhatt, pouting into her phone and taking selfies as usual. She does love to look at herself. Her little group of followers, Leila, Armani and Ayesha, copy her perfectly. Just behind them the **supremely annoying** Adil is arranging his stationery neatly on his desk. Milo, Govi and I sit down in our usual seats, which are as far away from all of them as is physically possible in our small classroom, but it's still not far enough.

"Oh, look, it's the losers again!" Beena announces gleefully as she looks up from her reflection.

Thankfully, just then our form teacher walks in. Beena and Manny and the other rule breakers quickly squirrel their mobiles and headphones away.

"Right, my little mathematicians, I hope we're wide awake and ready to be tested on our maths skills!" Mr Helix booms. He is a **big** man with a **big** voice and a **big** beard which constantly has bits of food in it. You can usually tell what he's been eating by the crumbs, which sounds gross, but he's actually a really nice teacher.

Although maths is one of my favourite subjects, a lot of kids don't like it, which makes it the lesson where the most trouble happens when the teacher's not looking. And if you're the kid who puts your hand up to answer a question, you may as well paint a target on your back for them to throw things at, because that's what happens.

"Anisha's ready, sir!" squeals Beena, and her followers laugh right on cue.

"Yes, well perhaps you could learn a thing or two from Anisha." Mr Helix peers over his glasses sternly at Beena.

I look at the floor, trying to ignore the sniggering and whispers of "**Teacher's pet**" from the front of the room.

"That's enough! Quiet now, or there will be extra algebra for everyone!" Mr Helix roars. "Right, before we tackle our weekly test, I thought we could warm up your brain cells with some problems which I will write on the board and you will work out on paper quietly. We'll share answers in five minutes. Go."

There's a rustle of backpacks being opened, pencil cases being unzipped and books being slapped onto desks while Mr Helix scrawls on the board:

STEVE HAD 15 BAGS OF 36 CARDS.
HE BOUGHT 11 MORE CARDS.
HOW MANY CARDS DOES HE HAVE NOW?

There are a few sighs and a bit of shuffling in

chairs as the class gets to work. I'm just happily starting to set out my workings when a shriek breaks the silence.

"RAAATTT!"

CHAPTER THREE

ARCH-ENEMIES EVERYWHERE!

As soon as the word **"RAT"** is shouted, **chaos** breaks out and kids are jumping onto their chairs and Mr Helix is trying to calm everyone down but no one's listening. I immediately glance at Milo, who is now **desperately** searching his very **empty** hoodie pocket. Oh no, Ralph has **escaped**! As I try to see what's going on across the classroom, I'm almost knocked over by Milo. He rushes past me to where Beena is smacking her bag against her chair and **thrashing** her arms and legs in all directions from her seat.

"Stop, you'll hurt him!" Milo yells, crossing his arms above his head for protection as he approaches a flapping Beena. She is balancing on her chair, arms rotating like two huge fans and her legs kicking side to side like a pendulum – it's a very odd and frightening sight and makes me think of a theory diagram I saw in a book once:

Just as I think things can't get any worse – "**What on earth...?**" barks the head teacher Mr Graft, who is suddenly standing in the doorway to our classroom. That stops everyone immediately, like a freeze-frame in a movie...apart from Milo, who swiftly retrieves his rat and silently slips Ralph behind his back.

"Would somebody explain to me why this class is being so disruptive? I can hear you from my office down at the other end of the corridor."

Mr Helix stands up to explain. "Well, er, I'm not quite sure, but it would seem someone spotted a **rat**...but, well, I can't see anything now."

"I can assure you there are no rodents in my school!" Mr Graft huffs. "Honestly, I think some of you children have very vivid imaginations. Let's try to use them in our story-writing, shall we, rather than causing a ruckus in maths? And, for goodness' sake, Beena Bhatt, would you kindly keep your arms and legs still, please, **this is not a gymnastics class**."

Hushed giggles come from the back of the classroom as Beena turns a funny beetroot colour and adjusts to a more normal sitting position.

While everyone is focused on Beena, and Mr Graft leaves us to it, Milo turns around and pops Ralph back into his hoodie pocket. "Please stay hidden this time, Ralph, not everyone loves rats. I know, **mad, right**? Tell you what, I'll make a deal with you. Stay in my pocket and you can have this nutty treat. What do you say?" Milo whispers to his rat. Ralph sniffs a little and then settles down in the pocket with his ratty snack.

"Right, shall we do some maths now? Unless anyone else feels the need to express themselves?" Mr Helix looks over his glasses at the class. I sneak a look at Milo and he mouths the word "**Phew!**" at me.

Everyone quietens down then and starts working on the maths problem. I carry on writing in my exercise book, but then I feel like someone is watching me. I glance up to see Beena Bhatt **glaring** at me, that way she always does when she thinks something's my fault. I'm in for it at some point then, as usual.

I look back down at the page and try to focus on the maths problem in front of me. Today has been eventful enough already. I really, **really** hope the rest of the day is going to be calm and drama-free!

Soon it's break time and we head out to the playground. We find a corner where it's quiet and Milo gets Ralph out to give him another snack to nibble on. Then he drags me to the library so he can borrow a book on how to take care of rats. We find one called **Rats, the Misunderstood Members of the Rodent World**.

After break time, we have art – well, sort of. Mr Helix wants us to practise drawing 3D shapes, but no one is listening. I turn my cube into a super science lab and Milo sketches a luxury rat mansion.

Platform + ladder

Nest

Wheel →

Ralph Chilling →

fluff

Govi draws the 3D shapes but gives them all weird, creepy faces. I want to ask him about it, but he scrunches the page up before the teacher can see and goes back to drawing plain ordinary shapes. I don't say anything then. I know he's had a hard time settling in at school and it can't be easy starting somewhere new. I think that's why he's so down sometimes.

Finally, at twelve o'clock, it's time for lunch. We check the menu as we walk into the dinner hall, even though I already know it's my favourite today.

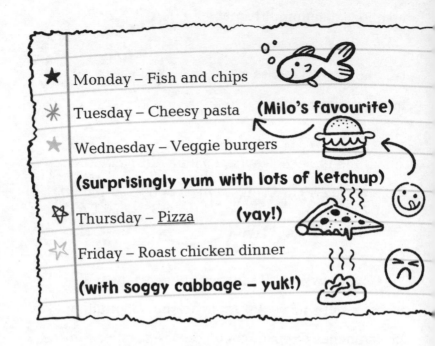

★ Monday – Fish and chips

✳ Tuesday – Cheesy pasta **(Milo's favourite)**

★ Wednesday – Veggie burgers

(surprisingly yum with lots of ketchup)

✪ Thursday – <u>Pizza</u>   **(yay!)**

☆ Friday – Roast chicken dinner

(with soggy cabbage – yuk!)

Milo and I go along the counter with our trays
and the dinner lady plonks two slices of pizza on
each of our plates. Then we head for our usual
"**losers**" lunch bench. The only other person who
sits on it apart from me and Milo is Govi.

"Hi, Govi. Ready to work on our experiment
later? I reckon we've got a good chance of **winning**."
Milo smiles.

"I kind of doubt that, Milo. I don't really win stuff." Govi shuffles his food round on his plate.

"Everything okay? You don't seem yourself," I say, concerned.

"Yeah, I suppose. I just…you know…I'm not sure about the project. Maybe, I should drop out and let you guys carry on. You did most of the building of it anyway, what with you two living on the same road."

"What? No, we've all worked so hard. You deserve an equal share of the credit, Govi," I say.

"Anisha's right, **we're a team**," Milo adds.

Govi looks up. "I guess."

"Good. So now let's get to figuring out how we can make our project even more awesome."

"I had an idea actually—" Govi starts to say quietly, but then Milo butts in:

"**Oh, oh, I know!** We can get some rocks from outside and—"

But before he can continue, the twins walk up to our table. **GREAT.**

"Hi, **Aniiiisha**!" Mindy sneers. "Did your mum tell you? We're coming to yours for dinner tomorrow night. Won't that be fun?"

I panic. "**What**? No one told me. Umm, well I might be busy, you know, things to do."

Milo nudges me. "I thought I was having dinner at yours tomorrow night? I've cleared it with Mum and everything. Your granny's making me some of those lovely **samosas**!" He's whispering, but not quietly enough.

Mindy claps her hands. "Oh, really? Isn't that lovely? It'll be like a big out-of-school **party**. You'll be there too, won't you, Govinder?" She smiles but it's **so fake**.

Govi blushes and shifts in his chair. "Umm, no, I don't live that close to Anisha...we're moving here but the house my parents bought isn't ready yet, so Mum drops me to school and picks me up and I... umm..." I cringe as Govi rambles.

"Haven't you been invited? How **awful** for you."

Mindy is enjoying this. "If you were our friend, we'd invite you over for dinner all the time, wouldn't we, Manny?"

Manny squints at us like he's trying to look mean, but it just looks like he can't see very well.

"Well, Govi already has friends. Us!" Milo protests. "He doesn't need you two!"

"Hmm, well, things change, you know. We'll just have to see," Mindy replies with **menace** in her voice, which makes my tummy **dip** like when you go over a big hill in the car.

Just as I think this conversation can't get any worse, who comes along but Beena Bhatt.

"Ah, look at this, are we having a **family gathering**?" She grins.

"No, we're **not** family," Mindy snaps.

"Now, now, I came to the wedding – your dad married Anisha's aunty. That makes you family," Beena insists.

Mindy goes red in the face. "**No. It. Doesn't,**" she says and then, just like that, she walks away. Manny looks a bit lost for a second and then follows her.

"**Touchy!**" Beena grins again and saunters away, twirling her hair.

"What was all that about?" Milo frowns. "I thought the twins and Beena were mates?"

"No idea." Govi shrugs but he's fiddling nervously with the **Geology Rocks** badge on his jacket and he has this **weird look** on his face.

"Don't be scared of them." I try to smile reassuringly, wishing – not for the first time – that it was that easy.

CHAPTER FOUR

IT ALL STARTS TO GO WRONG!

The afternoon goes by uneventfully, apart from another **rat emergency** during afternoon break where Milo thinks Ralph has escaped again, but it turns out he is just having a nap under a bit of torn-up newspaper in the bottom of Milo's pocket. When the bell goes at 3.20 p.m. and the school starts to empty, the three of us head over to the lab. Miss Bunsen is sitting at her desk when we get there, frowning at the pile of homework she is marking.

"Ah, right. Now, can I trust you children to carry on with your project while I just quickly pop round to Mr Graft's office? I won't be long and you know what to do if in doubt – safety first." She points to the poster on the wall that lists all the lab rules:

SAFETY FIRST!

- **ALWAYS** follow the teacher's instructions carefully

- **DO NOT** eat, drink or inhale anything used in science activities

- **ALWAYS** keep your hands away from your eyes, mouth and face during science lessons

- **ALWAYS** wash your hands after science activities, even if you have been wearing gloves

- **ALWAYS** use goggles when chemicals, glass or heat are being used in an activity

- **TELL** the teacher immediately if you have an accident during a science activity

- **YOU MUST ALWAYS** measure chemicals and other ingredients very carefully.
The wrong combinations or amounts can have **DANGEROUS** consequences

"Yes, miss," we reply together excitedly.

"I know I can trust you three." She smiles and walks off in the direction of Mr Graft's office.

"Come on, let's get our stuff out, there's so much to do. All our hard work is going to pay off if we just get this bit right," I remind both boys.

We've put so much effort into our project. It's the first time we've worked on anything together, all three of us. At first, we couldn't agree what to do. Milo wanted to create an ecosystem or an ant farm, as he says ants are the most **amazing** creatures on earth. But then we saw that's what Adil Ansa is making. So then Govi suggested making a rocket or a crane. Both sounded cool, but then I saw something online about making a **foam volcano** and we all agreed that was the one. So we found instructions and started experimenting.

HOW TO MAKE A VOLCANO

You will need:

- Empty plastic bottle with a wide neck or a clean glass jar
- White vinegar
- Washing-up liquid
- Food dye (red and yellow works well for lava)
- Bicarbonate of soda

1. Half fill the glass jar or bottle with white vinegar.

2. Add a good squirt of washing-up liquid, and a few drops of food dye.

3. Gently swirl the bottle or jar to mix the contents.

4. Place the bottle or jar onto a baking tray or dish…or this could get very messy.

★ 5. Now add a heaped teaspoon of bicarbonate of soda to the bottle or jar and wait for the volcano to erupt!

What's going on?

When you mix vinegar and bicarbonate of soda, it makes a gas called carbon dioxide. This forms bubbles in the vinegar. The bubbles of gas react with the washing-up liquid to make foam. The whole combination reacts so much that foam pours out – just like a volcano!

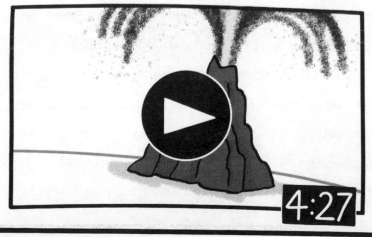

4:27

Crater

Throat

Ash Layers

Bedrock

Magma Chamber

We spent all our spare time over the last couple of weeks making this **awesome** papier mâché volcano to cover the plastic bottle that sits in the centre of it. We even created a cross section on one side of the model to show the different layers of rock and lava. That bit was my idea – I'm **so proud** of it.

Of course, like all good scientists, we wanted to test the experiment a few times in a spare container to make sure it works on the day of the science fair. So far, though, we've had mixed results – although we can get the volcano to erupt, we want the perfect explosion and that's been a bit tricky. Here's what happened...

Test 1: Apart from a funny smell, nothing happened for a bit – and then, just as we were going to give up, a big fountain of fizz shot up to the ceiling and back down again. **Maybe a bit too explosive?**

Test 2: There was a bit of fizzing and then a loud belching sound, but more of a **dribble** than an eruption.

Test 3 is today and we really need to get it right!

"I think we need more bicarbonate of soda," Milo says.

"Umm, I think we should proceed with caution," Govi warns us. "I'm going to get Miss Bunsen so she can supervise the exploding bit."

"Caution? **CAUTION** never won a science fair!" Milo shouts after him.

"Milo, we need to **concentrate**. Measuring the different components precisely is very important," I say as I snap on my blue protective gloves and plastic goggles. "We need to have this working by next week. We can't have any mistakes on the day of the science fair. And practice does make **perfect**! Right, let's at least do the first bit while we wait for Govi to come back with Miss Bunsen."

I pour the vinegar carefully into a spare container, watching that it doesn't drip down the side, and screw the cap back on the vinegar bottle when I'm done.

Milo gleefully squirts the washing-up liquid in,

chuckling to himself at the squelchy noise. Then he passes me the pipette and we add the food colouring, counting the ten drops together.

Now for the bicarbonate of soda. We only have a small amount in a plastic tub so I have to be careful not to waste or drop any. I'm just getting it out ready while we wait for Govi and Miss Bunsen, when there's a clattering **clang** and a loud **bang** outside the lab. Milo and I race into the corridor and turn left towards the noise. It's coming from inside the supplies room. I pull the handle down and the door swings open to reveal **Miss Bunsen**!

We quickly pull her up from the pile of science supplies she's fallen into. **Thankfully** she doesn't seem to be hurt.

"What happened?" I ask.

"I don't know. I popped in here to get some supplies ready for tomorrow's classes on my way back from seeing Mr Graft, but suddenly the door closed behind me and I couldn't get out! The handle on the inside has been broken for weeks so you can't turn it. I usually leave the stopper there so it stays open, but it must have got knocked out of the way!"

I look behind the door and around on the floor but there's no door-stopper. **Weird.**

Just then, there's a beeping sound and it suddenly starts **raining** in our school corridor! I quickly realize it's the sprinklers, which are like little showers that come on if the fire alarm is triggered. Even stranger, I smell **burned toast**! Who would be making toast now?

"Goodness me, it's all go today. We'd better follow procedure and get you two outside." Miss Bunsen starts to walk towards the exit.

I start to say, "We can't leave Govi," but then I see it. At first I think, **That can't be what I think it is**. But it keeps coming towards us and panic starts to bubble in my chest.

"Er, miss, I think you should turn around…" I murmur.

"We haven't got time for games, Anisha, come along. Actually, where is Govi? Is he in the lab still?"

"No, he went to look for you, miss – but seriously, you need to turn around **NOW**."

"What is it, Anisha? Oh!"

Coming out of the lab at an alarming rate is a very large, very foamy puddle of **bubbles**. The sprinklers are on full blast and so the puddle is getting rapidly bigger. I can just about see that inside the lab the floor is already **flooded** and there's foam and bubbles **everywhere**.

I don't understand. **How could this happen?** Miss Bunsen tries to investigate, but the foam river is **rising** and she ends up with what look like **foam ankle-boots** over her feet.

I grab Milo's arm and start to back away towards the exit. Govi comes running up then, out of breath and quite pink in the cheeks.

"Where have you been, Govi?"

"I couldn't find Miss Bunsen and I accidentally walked in on a meeting and got told off and then I needed the toilet! What's going on?"

"What's going on is that somehow our volcano experiment seems to have **EXPLODED** and now the sprinklers have come on and there's a **river of foam** flooding the lab and travelling out into the corridor!" I point frantically.

Miss Bunsen takes charge. "**Right**, children, no

more hanging around, I need to get you out into the playground – it's health and safety protocol. We can discuss the hows and whys once everyone is out. I imagine the **fire brigade** will be on their way now that the alarm is going off, so they'll be able to tell us exactly what's happened. Come along."

We wade along the corridor towards the exit, feet **sloshing** in the quickly rising foam flood. Voices echo as a few other teachers working late emerge from classrooms and offices, wondering what's going on. Just as I think it's not too bad, I spot a load of Petri dishes, pipettes and what looks like a long line of floating blue rubber hands drifting on the foamy river down the hallway. As we reach the exit door it suddenly flings open and standing there, looking **mightily unhappy**, is Mr Graft, the head teacher!

CHAPTER FIVE

CONSEQUENCES

"Does someone want to explain to me **what on earth** has happened here?" Mr Graft demands as a wailing fire engine pulls into the playground behind him. Milo, Govi and I sit on the wall, covered in foam and looking at our feet. Miss Bunsen tries to flick foam off her soggy shoes, but she does it a bit too hard and the foam lands on Mr Graft's face. He wipes it away with his finger and he looks even more annoyed now. Milo and I duck our heads and hope he doesn't notice us. Of course, that's not my luck at all.

"**Anisha Mistry**, is that you underneath all that foam?"

"Umm, yes, sir, it is me. There's been an, erm,

accident, I think. I'm not really sure what happened. We were just about to practise our foam volcano for the science fair and then we heard a noise and all of a sudden there was foam everywhere!" I stutter.

"Let me get this straight. You were experimenting with foam and now the school is covered in the stuff. I think we'd better take a look at this **volcano** you've made, don't you?"

"I know it looks bad, sir, but I **promise** we didn't even finish putting all the ingredients in, so how could it have been **us**?" I say, as two firemen **splosh** through the foam past us.

"Don't get smart with me, young lady." Mr Graft frowns.

Milo pulls himself up to face Mr Graft. "But she **is** smart sir, that's how you know she wouldn't have done this. I don't know what happened either, but it wasn't Anisha's or any of our fault."

I'm so glad Milo is my best friend.

Mr Graft doesn't look very **impressed**. "I'll decide who is or isn't responsible, Milo Moon. I think you'd better sit back down before you get yourself into more trouble!"

"But, sir…"

"Perhaps you'd better do as you're told, Milo," says Miss Bunsen.

Mr Graft nods and looks sternly at us all. "Thank you, Miss Bunsen. Right, now once the fire department have been and checked it is safe, hopefully they can look at where it all started and work out how."

I notice Govi is fidgeting next to me as if he's cold. "Are you okay?" I ask. "Do you want my lab coat?"

"N-n-no, I'm okay. Just shocked at how much foam there was." Govi shivers.

"I know, I just can't understand it," I say.

"I'm sorry I wasn't there to help," Govi says.

"It wasn't your fault, Govi. How could any of us have known what was going to happen?" Milo answers.

Just then a woman in a firefighter's uniform approaches us.

"So, what's the damage?" Mr Graft asks with a wince.

"Well, I'd say you've been **lucky**, really," the firefighter replies. "Could have been a lot worse. It's mostly stuff you can fix – wallpaper, displays. I think you'll have to close school for tomorrow and give it the weekend to dry out."

Mr Graft sighs loudly. "And where did it start? How did it start? Do we know yet?"

"Well, we'll need to investigate further, but I would say it started in the **science lab**," the firefighter answers grimly. She looks directly at us and continues. "You know you could have caused a lot worse **damage** and someone could have been **really hurt**."

Milo, Govi and I all hang our heads – until I remember we didn't actually do anything.

"B-but it wasn't—" I start, but Mr Graft cuts me off.

"I don't want to hear it, Anisha. I need to make some phone calls, not least to your parents. You three go with Miss Bunsen to the after-school club building and get cleaned up. I'll be over once I've finished here."

We have to walk back through the main building

past the lab to get to the after-school club. Miss Bunsen allows us to pick up our school bags from inside. Luckily they were on the side away from the volcano and didn't get attacked by all the foam. Govi and Milo grab theirs quickly, but I hover for a second. I can hardly bear to look at the **soggy mess** that was our experiment. Obviously we didn't do the test inside the papier mâché volcano, but the foam flood seems to have spread **everywhere** and run all across the table, soaking our outer volcano structure and turning it into a **floppy disaster**. I look at the floor instead, but there's so much foam and it niggles at me. Something's off.

Miss Bunsen interrupts my thoughts. "We'd better get a move on, Anisha."

We arrive at the after-school club, which is empty now. We're not there for more than a few minutes before Mr Graft turns up.

"I've called all of your parents," he starts and my tummy **dips**. "Anisha, I couldn't seem to reach yours, so I need you to give them this letter. Milo, your mother is waiting for you at home, I'll be meeting with her tomorrow. Govi, your mum is on her way here now." Mr Graft takes a deep breath. This can't be good. "Now, I don't take any pleasure from this, but I can't see how I can possibly allow you to continue to represent the school at the science fair. It's a matter of safety and our school's reputation."

"What do you mean, sir? We can still present our experiment, can't we?" I ask. My voice cracks and I blink so the tears don't come.

Mr Graft rubs the side of his head. "Look, there

will be other science fairs, but no, **you can't compete this time**."

"Now, Mr Graft, I'm sure we can come to some sort of compromise. They've worked so hard!" Miss Bunsen objects.

I look over at Govi. He's staring at the floor. Milo has gone very red in the face and is clenching his fists. I worry he'll make the situation worse, but he doesn't say anything. I don't really hear what else Mr Graft says – something about the decision being final and restrictions on use of the science lab. I just know it's the **WORST THING** that could ever happen.

After the lecture we say goodbye to Govi at the gates just as his mum's car pulls up outside the school. She glares at us and takes Govi by the arm back into the school to see Mr Graft. Milo and I head home in silence, **soggy** and a little **in shock** after what's just happened. I play it over in my mind and it still doesn't make sense. **How could our little volcano produce so much foam?**

I don't get long to think about it though, because as I walk into my house, the sound of Hindi music instantly fills my ears. Well, actually it's the sound of Aunty Bindi **warbling** badly over a Hindi movie soundtrack. I think for a split second about making a run for it to Milo's house, but it's **too late**. Aunty Bindi sways into the hallway and takes me by the

hands, dancing me into the living room. I say **"dancing"** but I'm not much of a dancer, so it's more of a **step-step-drag** situation.

Mum is sitting cross-
legged on her yoga mat
in the centre of the
room, while Bindi
prances me around
in a big circle.

"What's going
on? Aunty,
please can I
at least take my coat off?" I plead, pulling away.

"We're picking music for the party, **silly**!" Bindi
trills.

"I'm not really in a sing-songy mood, Aunty,
can't you get Uncle Tony to dance with you? That's
why you got married, wasn't it?" I slump **sulkily** in
my favourite comfy chair.

"**Sweetie**, what's wrong?" Mum looks up at me,
concerned. "Come here, give me your feet – your
aura is all blue and grey."

"No, Mum, **cleansing my aura** is not going

to help," I sigh, handing her the letter. "Mr Graft's been trying to call on your mobile. He left messages, didn't you get them?"

"No, **beta**, we've been listening to music. I didn't hear the phone, it might be on silent. Tell me, what's wrong?" she asks again.

"Just read the letter." I sigh louder.

Mum reads it and then looks up at me. "Is this **true**? Did you set off a **foam explosion** at school?"

"No, Mum, of course not! I don't know what happened but it wasn't me, **I promise**!" I protest.

"Oh dear. What will your dad say? He's on the board of governors. What would make you do such a **silly thing**? I don't understand, you're normally so careful with your science stuff."

"I told you, Mum! **I don't know what happened.** One minute we were just setting up to run a test for the volcano experiment and then we heard a noise, so we went to look and then…" I think of the scene in the lab after the foam explosion.

I think of all the foam on the floor and out in the corridor – **so much foam**. I pause and then I say it out loud for the first time. "What if it wasn't an accident, Mum? What if someone deliberately **sabotaged** us!"

"No, Anni, why would they? No one is out to sabotage you. Just admit you got it wrong. Maybe it was a **miscalculation**. Didn't you tell me you had problems the first two times you tried that experiment, so maybe you added too much of something this time?"

Mum's trying to be understanding but she doesn't get it.

"Anyway, this says we have to come into school tomorrow morning and have a meeting with your head teacher. Sounds serious, Anni. I need to think. **CHAI,** that's what we all need!"

Mum gets up to go to the kitchen. Apparently, tea makes everything better. Somehow, I'm not sure that will work for Mr Graft…

Just then, Granny Jas sneaks up on me – she always does that. "I heard what you just said, Anni. There's nothing else for it, we have to get to the bottom of this. I'm not having my granddaughter blamed for something she didn't do. What's the plan, **beta**?"

I turn to face Granny. "Plan? I have **nothing**, Granny. Mr Graft is sure it's my fault and now I'm not allowed to enter the science fair next week and it's so unfair, but I just don't think there's anything

I can do. I mean, I don't even know where I would start! I'm **totally baffled**, Granny!"

"So, let's get unbaffled, beta. Think! **Think hard!** Who would want to ruin your work like that and get you into trouble?"

"I don't know." I slump down in the chair and pull a face, feeling totally defeated.

"Oh no! Where is my **feisty** Anni? You don't just lie down and give up. I'm telling you, beta, stand up and others will stand up with you. Now, let me get you some **sabji** and **roti**. ˙

"You need your strength if you're going to start a serious investigation and take on these **science criminals**!" She punches the air with her tiny fist, grinning her toothless grin at me.

* Sabji is basically vegetable curry. Granny uses every and any kind of vegetable she can find. I'm not keen on some of them, like aubergine and spinach, but Granny always makes me try a bit. One of my favourites is cauliflower and potato – so yummy! And it's even yummier with chapatis, which is like a flatbread. Granny rolls them into perfect circles. I try to help sometimes, but mine turn out like a map of India.

"What? No, Granny, I'm not hungry, and I didn't say I was starting anything, I just…"

But it's too late, Granny has gone off to the kitchen and I'm left wondering yet again how I end up in these situations. Deep down though, I know Granny's right. I can't **do nothing** and just be **banned** from the science fair – it's too important. I have to **do something**. I don't know what yet, but I'll work it out. And **sabji** is good thinking food!

CHAPTER SIX

MUM AND DAD GET TOLD OFF!

By the time Dad gets home from work a bit later, I've got a full tummy and a **plan**. But first Mum calls a family meeting to discuss what's going to happen at school tomorrow. Dad has his **serious face** on and my stomach does somersaults as I sit down in my usual chair.

"What's wrong with your face? Anyone would think Anni had **BURNED** the school down! I don't know what all the fuss is about, it's just a little foam," Granny says to Dad.

"Mum, it's not a joke. And it wasn't just a little bit

of foam, it says in this letter the school was **flooded** with the stuff! The head teacher wants to see us!" Dad exclaims.

"**Pah**," says Granny, "the school probably needed a good clean anyway. And have you considered this might not be Anisha's fault at all? If that's the case, she will figure it out. She's very capable. You should know this! Honestly, I thought you knew our Anni better than that. You should be **ashamed** of yourselves!"

Dad's face goes a bit **pink** and he looks down at the floor. He doesn't like being told off by Granny. Then he sneaks a sideways glance at Mum and she looks back at him. She's got a funny expression on her face. There's a silent moment for what feels like for ever – and then they start **giggling**! Can you **believe it**?

70

"**I don't see what's so funny**," I say.

"Neither do I. It's very rude to laugh when you're being told off." Granny **humphs**.

"Sorry, Mum. Sorry, Anni, sweetheart." Dad turns to me, trying not to chuckle. "Okay, what happened, love? Tell me from the beginning."

So I do. I tell Mum and Dad **everything** and for once they listen carefully, nodding and then grimacing when I get to the bit about Mr Graft telling us off. When I'm done, Dad sighs and Mum says, "So, we'll go to the meeting tomorrow. Your dad and I will obviously speak to the head teacher and try to persuade him to let you enter the science fair. But if that doesn't work, what are you going to do about this?"

"**Me**?" I ask, unconvinced.

"Yes, **YOU**. Who solved the mystery of where Uncle Tony disappeared to before the wedding? Who always has a logical explanation for everything?" Mum asks.

That would be me. "Yeah, but—"

"'**Yeah, but**' nothing. You are very capable of getting yourself in – **and out of** – sticky situations. Whatever has gone on here – and we definitely don't think it was your fault, **beta** – you can find the truth."

"Wow, I wasn't expecting that," I say. "I thought you would **never** believe me."

"Well, I know we haven't always listened to you in the past and maybe that was wrong of us. We're not always right. We all make mistakes, Anni. Even grown-ups," Dad says.

Mum hugs me and Dad hugs Mum.

Granny says, "Right, now who wants some chai?"

The next day is Friday. The school has to stay closed for a clean-up, so of course the **fake news** that Milo, Govi and I caused a **foam explosion** in the science lab is bound to be everywhere on Monday.

Mum, Dad and I walk to school for the meeting with Mr Graft. Dad talks about what a lovely morning it is and Mum says something about cancelling the dinner we were meant to be having with Aunty Bindi and the twins later, but it feels like there's a stone in my stomach and I can't concentrate on what they're saying. I've never been in trouble at school before, **never**.

When we get to school, even I gasp as I see the damage from the **foam-plosion** to the floor and walls in the school hallways. There's a trail of foamy footprints, peeling wallpaper, and soggy posters have fallen down from the wall display. I hold my breath as we approach

Mr Graft's office. We almost bump right into Milo and his mum as they are leaving. Milo goes to say hello, but his mum speeds up and doesn't give us the chance to stop and speak. I guess he's in **a lot of trouble**.

I sigh, but before I can say anything Mr Graft pops his head out of his office and says **sternly**, "Ah, you'd better come in."

As we follow Mr Graft inside, even Dad looks a bit **scared**.

Mr Graft sits down in his chair and gestures for us to sit too.

"Right, Mr and Mrs Mistry. As you are aware, quite a **serious incident** occurred here at school yesterday. It seems, to my surprise, that young Anisha here and her lab partners were responsible for the **explosion of foam** which ran riot through the school."

"Now, wait a second. Are you **absolutely sure** Anisha and her friends were responsible?" Dad asks.

"Well, look, no one wants to believe good students like these could make such a mistake, but the evidence is **substantial**, Mr Mistry."

"I'm a lawyer, Mr Graft, as you know. I look at evidence all day. I just question whether this was a deliberate event, an accident, or whether something else has occurred here." Dad looks at Mr Graft questioningly and at the same time squeezes my hand.

"Sir, I assure you we are conducting a **full investigation** into how this incident occurred and—"

"Well, you call me back when you have concrete findings. Until then, as far as I'm concerned, my daughter is **innocent**," Dad declares and stands up.

All of a sudden Mum speaks up: "Mr Graft, I don't know much about science, but something bothers me about all this."

"Yes, of course, if I can explain anything, please ask away."

"You said there was a great deal of foam, yes?"

"Well, yes."

"It seems to me that to create that amount of foam, Anisha would have had to have access to a lot of **chemicals**. Or am I missing something? And I'm sure such a responsible school wouldn't allow the children to access large amounts of chemicals without **supervision**, would they?"

Mr. Graft
Headteacher

Mr Graft goes a bit **red in the face** then and **sputters**, "Well, of course not, but as I said the investigation is there to find out exactly what went on. Until we reach a final conclusion, I'm afraid I have to **enforce the ban** on Anisha's team entering the science fair."

"But—" I start.

"It's a matter of health and safety," Mr Graft firmly interrupts me.

Mum glowers at him. "I think you're being **very unfair**, Mr Graft," she says, squeezing my other hand. "But we can see you are not going to change your mind right now. Come on, Anisha, let's go home."

I don't understand grown-ups. One minute, Mum and Dad are sticking up for me, the next we're going home and I'm just supposed to accept that I can't take part in the **most important science fair** of my life so far **AND** that I'll miss out on the chance to win the trip to **the space centre**?!

I walk home with my head down, hands shoved in my jeans pockets.

"Don't pout, **beta**, that sulky face doesn't suit you," Dad says.

"Well I think I'm allowed to be **annoyed**, Dad. Why did you give up so easily? **I thought you guys were on my side**."

"We are and always will be on your side, **beta**, but Mr Graft is convinced and no amount of me jumping up and down or shouting at him is going to solve anything. I told Mr Graft he needs to prove you did it, but you can prove you didn't by finding out what really happened. **I believe in you**," Dad says.

I think for a second, and Granny's voice floats into my head as it often does: **Your brain is your super power**.

"I can do it. I'll find out who sabotaged our experiment and why, and prove it to Mr Graft before the science fair," I say.

"That's my girl." Mum smiles. "Family hug?" she says as she and Dad reach out.

I look around to make sure no one from school is nearby, then I snuggle in, just for a second.

CHAPTER SEVEN

VLOGGER GIRL

The weekend goes by in a blur and, before I know it, **it's Monday again**. I walk up Bell Lane alone. Milo's mum has walked him to school this morning. I guess she must think I'm a **bad influence** now.

When I get there, just outside the gates there is a boy with a camera on a tripod and a girl holding a clipboard in one hand and her phone in the other. They're both older than me and wearing the uniform of the secondary school up the road – black blazer with a yellow and green tie. The girl looks **familiar** though. For a second I think I might know her, but how could I? They try to talk to a few of the parents dropping off younger kids, but mums and dads in a rush don't stop for anyone. I'm so glad I'm allowed to walk to school by myself now. I didn't mind so much when Granny Jas used to pick me up, but Mum was **totally embarrassing**, trying to make friends with kids from my year and asking me if I liked any of the boys – **urgghh**! She even started a morning meditation circle in the playground with some of the other mums. I had to pretend I didn't know her, **I just couldn't even**.

Anyway, as I get closer and look more carefully at the girl, I realize where I know her from – she's that **Veena**, the vlogger who everyone likes. Her vlog is called **V Versus the World**. She makes videos about all kinds of everyday things and puts them online. Mostly it's her opening free stuff she gets sent – boring! **What's she doing outside our school?** I wonder, as my tummy does a somersault and not in a good way. Then, to make things worse, I see Beena Bhatt in her bright pink jacket with the fur collar. She's standing with her mates, chatting to the vlogger girl. I cross my fingers and duck my head down, hoping she doesn't speak to me as I go past them.

"I'm sorry, did you say you were taking part in the science fair or not?" the vlogger girl asks Beena wearily.

"What? **No**!" Beena **snaps**. "Why would I want to do that? I have a life, you know! Come on, you lot, we need to go and check my hair before class." And with that she marches off, her three underlings scuttling behind her. As they pass me, Beena points in my direction. "Oh, look it's one of the science dummies, that's who you want to talk to! They know all about the **foam flood**, don't you!" she shouts out smirking.

Veena looks over at me. "Hello, do you go to this school?"

"Umm, yes…" I say, not quite stopping. I notice she is grinning at me **slightly scarily**.

"We heard the fire service had to be called to the school on Thursday due to an **explosion** in the science lab. What exactly do you know about it? Were you here **when it happened**? How do you feel about that? Has it **disrupted** your life? What will happen if the science fair **doesn't go ahead** later this week?

Do you think it will ruin your education and possibly your whole future? Tell the viewers of my vlog what this has done to you. The **powers-that-be** need to answer for your pain, don't they? Who masterminded the attack of foam on your school? What do you know about the mysterious substance that seemed to be blocking the drains and seeping out of the main entrance on Thursday?" She grabs the camera off the tripod and thrusts it in my face.

"**Er, I have to get to class, sorry**," I stutter, and stumble through the school gate.

"Oh drat," I hear Veena saying. "I thought this was going to make a great story for my vlog. I'm sick of opening boxes and squealing, '**Ooh, look!**' I'll never be a famous journalist at this rate. I need a big story to be taken seriously!"

The boy with the tripod mutters something about all this standing around not being worth a fiver – but before I can worry any more about them, I spot Mindy and Manny heading straight for me!

"Hi, Anisha," they say at exactly the same time, which really **creeps me out**.

"Hi, Mindy. Hi, Manny," I answer nervously, looking around for help.

"We were disappointed that Friday's dinner was cancelled, but of course we understand. You must have been in **BIG** trouble after the **INCIDENT**. So, what did that girl want?" Mindy narrows her eyes at me.

"Nothing. I mean, she wanted to talk about the school being closed on Friday."

"Well, I hope you didn't tell her anything. You could get yourself into even more trouble for that, you know. Your perfect record is already tarnished. Such a shame." Mindy smiles her **Cheshire Cat** smile at me and Manny nods behind her.

"I didn't say anything, actually, but why are you so bothered?" I challenge them, suddenly feeling a surge of bravery. **Where did that come from?** I instantly wonder.

"Hi, Neesh, don't you need to get to the library before class?" Milo asks cheerfully as he appears at my side. "You know, to do the thing?"

Manny looks confused and Mindy glares at us both, before **hissing**, "We'll be seeing you later then."

"Thanks, Milo," I say, once they're out of earshot.

"What for? We really do have to get to the library if you want to get that science magazine you've been banging on about!"

"Er, before I go anywhere with you, where is that rat of yours, Milo?"

"Don't worry, I realized keeping him in my pocket wasn't that safe, so I came up with a better idea!" Milo turns to show me his backpack, which, now I look, seems kind of rectangular. I carefully unzip the top of the bag to see the most **extraordinary** hutch inside! Milo has made it very cosy, with a lining of torn-up newspaper, and even attached a water bottle, a small feeder and a little wheel for Ralph, so it's like a mobile home for a rat. Ralph looks up at me and tilts his head slightly.

I give him a little wave, then zip Milo's bag up again. "Very nice, Milo. Are you planning on keeping him in there all the time? It seems a bit dark."

"Actually, rats **prefer** the dark," Milo tells me.

"Okay, well just make sure he doesn't get out again, Milo. Although watching Beena Bhatt thrash around like that the other day was quite funny," I say, giggling.

We head to the library to see if Mr Bound the librarian will order me in a copy of the latest **Young Scientist Monthly**. He is so helpful, he even tells me about a new book on science theories that is coming out and says he'll order a copy in. Milo asks about books on famous rats, which makes Mr Bound smile. "Hmm, that might be a tricky one, Milo. Let me have a little search and see what I can find."

I check my watch – it's only 8.36 a.m. so we have fourteen minutes until the bell goes for registration. We grab a table in the corner of the library by the history books, where no one really goes.

"What did your mum and dad say about the accident, Neesh? My mum was going **mad** at me all weekend and I missed out on your granny's cooking on Friday. I was **gutted**!"

"You'll never guess, Milo – Mum and Dad believed me. They tried to stick up for me, but Mr Graft wouldn't listen. We're still not allowed to take part in the science fair! So it's up to us, Milo. **We have to find out what happened!**"

"But I still don't get it, Neesh. We only turned our backs for a minute. How can an accident happen when you're not even in the room?"

"Exactly!" I hiss. "It wasn't an accident, Milo. I think someone set us up. Don't you think **it's a bit funny** that at the exact moment we leave the room to investigate a noise in the hallway, the volcano **erupts** without us even touching it?"

"I guess, but who could have done it? There was no one around!"

"I don't know, but I'm going to find out. I can't have this on my school record – it's not fair because it wasn't our fault. Granny Jas says you have to

stand up for yourself when you've been wronged, so that's what I'm doing."

"Okay, I'm in. We should make a list of suspects, right?"

"Right!" I grab my notepad and a pencil from my bag and write:

FOAM-PLOSION – LIST OF SUSPECTS

I stare at the blank page. Where do we even start? Then I see him. Of course, it's so obvious! I nudge Milo to look where I'm looking – **Adil Ansa**, our biggest rival for the science fair competition, is standing just across the library in the line for the librarian's desk.

"Adil? You think he's the one? It makes sense, I guess. Would he be so mean, though?" Milo whispers.

"I don't know, but I **DO** know that he really doesn't want to lose. He might be ready to do anything to stop us from winning," I say.

As Adil approaches the librarian, Milo and I duck out of our seats and sneak up to listen in.

"Returning these, please." He heaves the heavy science books he's carrying across Mr Bound's desk. As he does that, I notice the picture on the top book is of a **volcano**!

Mr Bound scans the label on the inside cover and tells Adil, "It looks like you have only had them a week, you can keep them another week if you need to."

"No, it's okay, I got what I needed out of them."

Milo and I look at each other.

"He got what he needed? Like **how to make a foam explosion**!" I whisper.

"You don't know that for sure!" hisses Milo, but Milo's idea of a whisper is not everyone else's idea of a whisper. Truthfully, Milo only has one volume level and it's **LOUD**!

Adil turns round to see where the noise came from. Mr Bound looks over and so do the eight other kids in the library.

"This is a library, not a train station. We don't have to be silent, but you will kindly keep the noise down!" hisses Mr Bound.

We creep back to our table with the eyes of the whole library on us, including Adil, who **glares** at us.

A few minutes later Milo and I are in the corner debating what our next move should be, and whether Adil would really have **sabotaged** our experiment to knock us out of the competition, when Adil himself pops up from behind a shelf, **teeth gritted** and **nostrils flaring**.

"If you're going to accuse someone of something, at least have your facts straight."

"I, umm, well, what do you think we're accusing you of?" I retort.

"I just heard exactly what you said, about trying to pin that **ridiculous** foam explosion on me. I have a reputation to keep up, you know, I won't have my good name slandered. **AND** you come here to accuse me? I'm a library monitor, you know, are you trying

to get me fired? Plus, if my parents get news of this accusation, they'll be furious. I'm a **straight A** student, as you well know, Anisha Mistry." Adil huffs and folds his arms.

"Okaaay, man, **chill**, I think we just need to…" Milo raises his hands and leans back in his chair as he speaks, knocking into the bookcase behind him. Unfortunately, he dislodges a very haphazard stack of books which is piled on the shelf. Books are sent sliding every which way, while the three of us look on **in horror**.

Milo scratches his head. "Wow, well that was a daft place to leave them!"

"Can't you two just go away now?" Adil mutters. "The library was my **happy place** until you showed up."

"Not until you answer one question," I say.

"I didn't sabotage your stupid experiment, if that's what you want to ask," Adil snaps as he starts picking up books from all around us.

"So where were you at 3.25 p.m. on Thursday then?"

"If you must know, I was **rehearsing**," Adil retorts.

"Rehearsing? Yeah, okay," I say, **unconvinced**.

"Science isn't my only passion, actually. I have other interests."

"Really?" Milo and I say at the same time.

"Yes, really. You shouldn't just assume things

about people, you two. I joined the **drama club** a few weeks ago and I have been cast in the very **important** and **integral** role of villager number four in the school performance of **Beauty and the Beast ACTUALLY**!! I have my script in my bag if you don't believe me."

Milo and I look at each other, eyebrows raised. **Is this for real?**

"I can see you don't believe me, so let me demonstrate," he declares. "'Oh, I am wounded! The beast struck me, my heart…

aaaaahhhh!'" Adil staggers backwards dramatically, clutching his chest.

I cover my eyes. I think we've made a huge mistake!

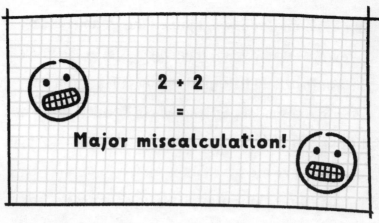

2 + 2

=

Major miscalculation!

"I'm so sorry, Adil," I start, but Adil rolls his eyes and waves my apology away.

"Don't make a fuss, Anisha. I can see how you'd think I'd want you out of the way, but **truthfully** I quite like having some competition. It would be boring to be the best at everything all the time!" He smiles.

Just then the bell goes and it's time to head to registration. We quickly tidy up the rest of the fallen books and leave the library.

"Hmm, so it wasn't Adil. I'm confused," Milo grumbles as we walk to our classroom.

"I think we should go back to our list," I say,

pulling out my notepad. I write Adil's name and cross it out.

~~Adil Ansa~~

I think for a second and then write:

The twins
Beena Bhatt

Milo is looking over my shoulder. "How can it have been Beena or the twins? Beena Bhatt was being picked up at 3.20 p.m. by her chauffeur. And the twins had the dentist, **remember**?"

He's right, we've got nothing.

"Well, it might still be worth checking them both out," I say unconvincingly. "I don't know who else it could be, Milo. We need **clues**, **evidence**. Good scientists find **proof** to back up their theories."

"Okay, well the science lab is still closed because

of the clean-up, so maybe we can sneak in at break time and look for clues?"

"**Great idea!** Now let's get to class before we're late," I say.

On the way I notice someone peering in through one of the windows of the science lab. As we get closer, I realize who it is – it's the vlogger girl from earlier. **What is she up to?**

CHAPTER EIGHT

SOGGY CLUES

At break time we head to the **science lab** to look for **clues**. The caretaker Mr Bristles is just outside by the supplies cupboard, putting a new handle on the door.

"Here they come, the **foam fiends**!" he chuckles.

"Hi, Mr Bristles, we're so sorry if you had to clean all that up. We did offer, but Mr Graft said we'd probably make it worse," Milo apologizes.

"Well I'm not sure that would be possible, young man. There was so much of it. I mean, **how on earth** did you get it all the way down the corridor so quickly? Left me a right load of work, it did.

Don't worry, I think I know you two well enough to be sure you didn't mean to **explode foam** all over the school. I did think it was **odd,** though, that you'd make a **mistake** like that. But I guess even perfect students get it wrong sometimes, eh?" Mr Bristles grins. Ever since we saved him from his office after the twins locked him in earlier this year, he's been a lot less grumpy with us. I don't think he and the twins have made up yet, though.

"Well, Mr Bristles, we came looking for **clues** actually – you know, to see exactly what mistake led to the **explosion**. I can't understand how it could have happened and I have a funny feeling someone else was involved. Would it be okay if we checked over our volcano?" I ask.

"Sure, it's still in the lab. I moved it to the corner – well, what's left of it. I'm off to find a better screwdriver. Try not to cause too much trouble, will you?" he jokes.

Milo and I enter the lab and approach the **pile**

of mulch that used to be our science experiment. I have to blink a couple of times. I don't cry very often, but we put so much hard work into this project and now it's **ruined**. The big container we were testing the experiment in has been placed next to the spoiled volcano, still half full of foam.

"Well, I guess we need to see if there's anything in the container that shouldn't be there." I wince.

"Okay, shall we?" Milo grins **enthusiastically** as we grab some blue gloves out of the box on the side and put our hands in.

"This is gross," I say, while also secretly quite enjoying the **squelching**.

"I feel something!" Milo yells.

"Er, yes, that's my hand!"

"Oh, sorry, I wondered why it was moving."

"Wait, what's that?"

"What?"

"This!" I say **triumphantly** as I pull out a sticker. It's one of those plastic 3D stickers. It's a bit soggy

and a bit faded, but round and blue and says **Star of the Week** on it.

"Oh," says Milo, disappointed. "That's Govi's, isn't it? He was **Star of the Week** in last week's assembly."

"Yeah, I think you're right." I sigh. "It must have dropped off his jumper when we were setting up the test. Keep looking."

"Where is Govi anyway?" Milo points out. "Shouldn't he be **helping** us?"

"I heard one of the office staff telling Mr Helix that Govi is sick at home," I answer.

"Oh, okay, I hope he feels better."

We carried on **squelching** for a bit longer.

"I don't think there's anything else in here, Neesh. What now?"

I realize he's right. There are no clues here. What was I thinking? "We can't do this alone, Milo, we need help. Someone, somewhere knows what happened here."

"We need witnesses!" says Milo, looking pleased with himself.

"Yes! **Witnesses!** How do we get the word out that we're looking for information though?" I wonder. And then I realize. "Milo, I met someone outside school this morning who likes investigating **AND** has the ability to help us get a message out to potential witnesses!"

"Who?" Milo looks confused.

"**Veena the vlogger!** We can ask her to let us post a video message online appealing for help – maybe we could even offer a **reward**? I'm not sure what, but we should definitely speak to her. She said she wanted a real story for her vlog, and we can give her a real story! If we can get a message to her somehow, she might come back to the school.

But how do we get in touch with her?"

"I've got an **idea**," Milo says. "We've got computer club at lunch, we can try to get onto Veena's website and send a message on the contact page."

"Milo, that's **genius**!" I say, just as the bell goes for the end of break. "Right, we know what we need to do later, let's get back to class."

CHAPTER NINE

GOING VIRAL

During computer club at lunchtime, Milo distracts the teacher by telling her all about his idea for a new computer game set in a rat kingdom. She listens to him waffling on about all the different levels it would have, while I go onto **V Versus the World** and hit the **CONTACT ME** button to send Veena an instant message. I hope she reads it in time.

The rest of the day goes by **uneventfully** and **extremely slowly**. Last lesson is geography, but I can't concentrate and keep looking out of the window. From this angle I can just about see the school gates. The clock in our classroom ticks loudly as everyone else hunches over their maps. I sneak a look out of the window again and that's when I see her. **She's here!** I nudge Milo – it worked, Veena must have got our message!

At home time, we decide it might look a bit suspicious if we just walk right up to Veena, and we don't want any of the kids or teachers to see us in case that tips off the **real culprit,** so we hang back for a few minutes until the school playground is pretty much empty. Veena's lurking by the gate with that boy and his tripod when we finally leave the main building.

"Hi, remember me? I'm Anisha. You're Veena, aren't you?" I say **cheerfully**, sticking out my hand as I walk up to her.

"Oh yes, the girl who didn't want to talk," **grumbles** Veena. "So, I got your message, I'm here, and this had better be something good. I had a free study period and I was in the middle of some **important** research!"

"Well, umm, yes." I look at her clipboard – it's decorated with a large **V** made from stick-on jewels. "I'm sorry, Veena. I was in a rush to get into school this morning – you know we missed a day on Friday and I was just so keen to get back and learn something." I grin the widest grin I can. Veena looks at tripod boy and rolls her eyes in **disbelief**.

"Right, so you want to give me an interview now then? Have you actually got any information I can use that people at home will be interested in?" She yawns.

"Well, we kind of need your help actually. The **foam incident** you want to know about – we think it was **sabotage**," I say carefully.

All of a sudden Veena looks very interested. "Sabotage? Okay, tell me more."

So we do. We tell Veena about the **foam-plosion** and how weird it was that there was so much foam so quickly. We tell her about our investigation and how we've come to a **dead end**.

We need witnesses to come forward – someone must know something.

Veena nods a lot as we talk; she makes notes on her clipboard and frowns as she concentrates. Eventually, when we've stopped **babbling**, she says, "So who else is on your list now you know this Adil Ansa didn't do it?"

I blush. "Well that's the thing, our other suspects both have **alibis** – which we'll check out of course!" I add as I see Veena raise her eyebrows.

"Okay, so you really need more information. This is what we're going to do then. We need to get your faces online and appeal for information. My followers are **loyal** and **nosy**, they will want to help!"

She clicks her fingers at the tripod boy, who looks like he's falling asleep. He jumps up to point the camera at Milo and me.

"So firstly, can you both tell everyone at home what your names are?"

"I'm Milo Moon and this is my friend Anisha Mistry." Milo points at me. I grimace and do a really awkward half-wave at the camera. **Nice one, Neesh!**

"So, Milo, Anisha, your school was closed for the day on Friday, can you tell me why? Was it because someone is intent on shutting down your school? Is there a conspiracy here? Should parents be worried?"

Veena really does want a story! "Well," I start nervously, "it might have been **sabotage**. We're not sure, but we're following up **clues** and that's where your viewers come in. We need their **help**."

"Right, okay and how can they help?" Veena nods at me.

"Well, if they go to our school and saw something, **anything suspicious** last Thursday around home time, please let us know."

Just then I notice Milo's backpack **wiggling** next to his feet. I remember Ralph is still in there and try to get Milo's attention as he talks to Veena and the camera all about the foam flood. Then I try and reach the backpack by sliding my foot across, but it's too far and still moving.

Milo continues talking and neither he, Veena, nor tripod boy notice the wriggling that seems to be going on in Milo's bag.

"So…" Veena smiles. "Is there anything else you can tell us about the **foam flood**?"

Before either of us can answer, the wriggling backpack **falls over** right by Veena's feet.

"Sorry about that," apologizes Milo. "He's probably looking for food."

"Who is?" Veena asks, her eyebrows now raised again.

"I'll show you!" Milo answers cheerfully.

"Um, Milo, now might not be the right time," I warn.

I try to grab Milo and leave, but he's already unzipping the backpack. "Now," he says, "we must be gentle, as Ralph is a little **nervous** around new people, so let me just explain to him who you are."

I stifle a smile as Veena looks from Milo to me, completely **baffled**.

Milo dips his head right into the backpack and whispers, "Don't worry, this is a nice lady, stay calm, little Ralph. Let's get you out for some fresh air, **come on**."

Things happen in **slow motion** then – Veena turns

away for a moment to say something to the tripod boy and so doesn't see Milo place Ralph on her clipboard, which she's holding away from her. She must feel his weight though, because suddenly with a jerk she looks down, **SHRIEKS** and, in the same moment, flings her hands upwards, sending poor Ralph into a **double somersault**! He recovers quickly though and somehow lands feet first in Veena's **hair**. She **screams** even louder this time!

   "**Get it off, get it off,** where is it, I can feel it gnawing on my scalp, get it off, Charlie, I mean it, **GET IT OFF ME**!" She starts hitting herself in the head while Charlie the tripod boy just stands shocked for a second. Then Veena screams again and he jumps into action, **sort of**.

Veena writhes about on the floor, trying to get Ralph out of her hair – which, by the way, now looks like a **bird's nest**.

Charlie scrambles to help her with one hand, but also makes sure he points the camera right at her to capture the **hilarious** action. Just then Milo notices a light on the camera and says, "Cool, is that **live-streaming** to the internet? We might go **viral**!"

Once things had calmed down, we got talking to Veena properly off-camera. She really wants to be an **investigative journalist**, so she goes round trying to solve local mysteries. The whole reason she came to our school in the first place was because she heard about the **foam-plosion** from her cousin on Friday when the school was shut, so she decided to come and check it out. Apparently when she got here Mr Graft said, "Oh, you must be mistaken, **no explosions here**, but please do report on our science fair as it's so very interesting!" Veena didn't think that was **half** as interesting as a **foam-plosion conspiracy** (as she's calling it). She wanted to see if there was something more intriguing to report on, so that's why she was being so nosy, peering in windows and asking lots of questions.

Then she told us about one of her last investigations, when she was reporting on a

runaway tortoise that had escaped from a local nursery. Milo got all **excited** and offered to join the search-and-rescue team, but Veena said not to worry, they'd found old Turbo wandering down Market Street, happy as can be. Then Milo said, "Did you know tortoises sometimes eat their own poo?" And that, not surprisingly, was the **end** of **that** conversation!

Slowest animal
+
gross poo fact
=
Fastest end to
a conversation ever

CHAPTER TEN

AUNTY BINDI'S BEAUTY SHOW DISASTER

When I get home a little while later, it's almost ten minutes past four and the house is quiet, apart from the low noise coming from the telly.

"Is that you, **Anni beta**?" Granny Jas calls from the living room.

"Um, yes, be there in a sec," I say, smoothing down my school skirt and brushing off a bit of **rat fur**.

"Ah, Anni, did you have a good day?" Mum asks as I walk into the living room. Dad's there with a **funny look** on his face and Granny is **laughing** at the telly, which is **weird** because normally she only watches the news and her Indian dramas, which are not funny at all. I turn to see what's so funny and realize they are watching the local news. On the screen is the headline **RAT ON THE RAMPAGE IN LOCAL SCHOOL GOES VIRAL** underneath a close-up shot of Milo holding his rat, while Veena desperately scrubs her head, face and body in the background. Looks like we did go **viral** – and so much for Ralph the **SECRET** rat!

Luckily Mum, Dad and Granny think it's quite funny that we ended up on the local news. All I can think, though, is that we are back to the beginning. Veena told us to keep looking for clues and to suspect **everyone**. But there's, like, **357** kids in our school (if you don't count me, Milo and Govi) – it would take **for ever** to investigate them all.

I go to my room and think and think until **my head hurts**. Then, later that evening, Aunty Bindi comes over and my head hurts **even more**! Aunty Bindi used to live with us, but since she married Uncle Tony earlier this year she lives with him and the twins, Mindy and Manny. She still spends every spare minute at our house, though, especially recently, what with all the party plans for Granny Jas's **seventy-fifth birthday**. Aunty Bindi **loves** a family celebration. Any excuse for balloons, sparkly decorations and a marquee!

We're all in the living room when she comes in, huffing and puffing, arms full of **glossy pink** shopping bags – the kind you get when you buy something **expensive**. Uncle Tony comes in after her, weighed down with boxes in the same glossy pink.

"What **on earth** is all this?" Granny **exclaims**.

"You're going to love it!" Bindi squeals.

"I don't know why there's so much of it!" grumbles Tony, but then Bindi gives him a **gooey look** and he smiles.

"But anything for my **sweetheart**. Anyway, better be going, the twins are with my mum and dad, so I need to get over there and pick them up. I'll see you at home later, **honeykins**?" He passes the boxes on to Granny, who is surprisingly strong. She plonks the boxes in the marquee, which Aunty Bindi insisted we have attached to the back of the house. We had one for her wedding and there's almost as many guests coming to this party now she's in charge!

"Yes, **sweetums**. Oh, and make sure the children use that mouthwash the dentist gave them on Thursday. He said it was very important for their gums."

Ah, so they *were* at the dentist then, I think to myself. That means they definitely couldn't have been in school setting me up. I slump in my cosy chair. They weren't **proper** suspects, but it just reminds me that I don't have any **real** ones.

"Everything okay, Anni?" Bindi hands me a couple of bags. "Come on, you can help me with all this **exciting stuff**. This party is going to be **AMAZING**!" she says as she blows a goodbye kiss to Uncle Tony. I pull a face and say, "No, thank you, I need to figure some stuff out."

"What could be more important right now than our family celebration?" Bindi shakes her head in **disbelief**.

"She's having a difficult week," Mum whispers over my head.

"Well, sometimes doing something different can be a good distraction. Come on, Anni, I really need your help. This party isn't going to arrange itself. I found these **ultraviolet** decorations that change colour under a special light, and I got **loads** of matching stuff, even UV nail polish for us to wear!

You **know** you want to help me – we have so much fun together usually! And there's banners to make – so many jobs to do, so little time. Say you will help, **pleeeeeeeeeeeeeeeeeeeeeeeeeeeeeeeeeeeeease**?"

I don't mean to lose my temper right then, but something **snaps** inside me. I just need some quiet to think and I can't do that with Aunty Bindi going on and on. I stand up, sending my book spinning across the floor. I realize straight away I've probably gone too far already, but my head feels like it's going to **EXPLODE** and the words just **FLY** out of my mouth.

"Look, Aunty, no one cares about this **stupid party** – why can't you see that? Granny doesn't even want a big fuss, but you **always** do this – you don't listen! Just leave me alone, will you? Some of us have **actual real-life problems**."

Mum and Dad seem frozen in time. Granny pops her head round the kitchen door. Bindi stares at me, open-mouthed. I stomp off upstairs, not caring if

anyone follows me, even though I
know for a fact that **someone** will.

My tummy swirls **horribly**
and I'm not surprised when a few
minutes later there's a knock on my bedroom door.
I really did go too far, didn't I?

"Can I come in, Anni? I'm sorry about not
listening. I'm listening now if you want to talk
to me," a soft voice says through the door. Bindi

opens the door and sticks her head round, smiling **hopefully**.

"I suppose." I roll my eyes and sit up, crossing my legs. Bindi sits down on the edge of my bed, fiddling with the edge of my stars-and-planets blanket, waiting for me to speak.

"**I'm just fed up**." I shrug.

Bindi holds my hand. "Talk to me about what happened. You've always been able to talk to me – even when you didn't want to tell your parents what was bugging you, you used to run to me and I'd make it better. I might not be able to make it better now, but I can listen."

So I talk. I tell Aunty Bindi about **how the experiment went wrong** when no one was in the room, and how Mr Graft was so **angry** that he banned our group from entering the science fair. I tell her how we went looking for clues and eliminated Adil, and enlisted the help of Veena the vlogger girl. Aunty Bindi tries not to chuckle when

I tell her about Milo's rat going **viral** and even I can't help smiling.

"So," I say, "we're no closer to finding out who set us up, but I just know **someone** did, Aunty."

"Then you don't give up, Anni. Did you know that when I was at college I got the blame for something I didn't do?"

I look up then, surprised. "No, what happened?"

"Well, it was actually in sixth form when I was seventeen and attending a beauty course. I was the **star student** in the class, you know!"

"**Wow!** So how come you got the blame for something?"

"There was a big end-of-year beauty show with judges and a catwalk and everything. Each of us students had a model to work with and we had to do their hair, nails and make-up. I was so **excited**. Everyone said I was sure to win. But there was another girl, Seema...I don't know why or how, but she just decided she didn't like me and **that was**

that. You know you can try to be nice to everyone, but some people are just that way."

I nod, thinking about Beena Bhatt and the twins.

"Anyway, it was the day before the **big show** and I remember getting my workstation ready with all my brushes and palettes. I was planning to use this new spray-on hair dye on my model, so I lined up all of my stuff ready for the morning so I could work quickly." Bindi frowns at the memory. My stomach feels funny and I know **something bad** is going to happen in the story.

"The next day we all got to work on our models. But the lipstick on my workstation was the wrong colour – not the gold I'd picked but a bright pink. **Okay**, I thought, **never mind, I'll make it work**. Then the eye pencil had snapped and it was too short to even sharpen it again. Everyone else's models were almost ready and I started to **panic**. 'Quick,' I said to my model, Amaira. 'I just need to spray on the colour for your hair.' So I did. It was meant to be a peacock-blue streak, dramatic and bold. It was going to be the final touch to a fantastic look. Instead the spray came out **frothy** at first and then it was a **fluorescent** orange colour. It spluttered and instead of being a clean, bold streak, it was a **splattery mess** all over Amaira's hair and on her face. My look was **RUINED**."

"**Oh no!**" I gasp.

"**Oh yes**, and my teacher wasn't impressed.

I lost **loads** of marks for my final result, all the models went onto the catwalk except mine and you can guess who won first prize."

"**Seema**," I say, horrified. "Did you tell anyone you thought she **sabotaged** you?"

"Yes, I tried, of course. No one **believed** me. They thought I just made a silly mistake and didn't want to own up to it. I wish now I'd proven it to everyone and cleared my name like you're trying to do. Don't let anyone tell a lie about you, Anni, trust me. You've got this, you can **outsmart** anyone."

"I don't know," I start, but Bindi cuts me off.

"You do, Anni, you **do** know – **believe in yourself**! If you say someone sabotaged your experiment, think about who would want to do that and why. The answer is in that head of yours **somewhere**, you just have to find it. Your brain is **super-strong**, you'll figure it out." She smiles and ruffles my hair. I usually hate that sort of thing, but today I don't mind so much.

"Right, **young lady**, are you going to help me put up some decorations for this party now or what?" Bindi **teases**.

"Yes, yes, I suppose so," I laugh. "If I must." And we head out of my room onto the landing.

"Good, because the party is in a few days and there is **so much to do**! I have to leave again in an hour because your uncle is taking me and the twins to dinner with his client Mr Bhatt and his family. You know the daughter, I think? Beena, is it?"

I freeze. "Sort of, yes. Just watch the twins carefully around her, Aunty."

Aunty Bindi laughs. "Don't worry, the twins have been much better lately and Beena seems very **sweet**. I saw her only the other day in the school playground – they all seemed very friendly together."

"Yeah, they are friendly – a bit **too** friendly! Just out of interest, what day was that?" I ask, as a funny and familiar **feeling** rises in my tummy.

"Umm, Thursday, I think? Yes, it was, because the twins had the dentist – that's why I was picking them up. Anyway, I was running a bit late. Tony's chauffeur, Mustaf, had the day off, so I drove myself and you know what I'm like with all the roundabouts and zebra crossings round there. When I eventually got there after a few little detours, the twins were waiting in the playground, talking with Beena. I did offer to drop her home, as she was carrying a big case, but she said she was fine."

I blink twice, absorbing this information. A big case… Hanging around after school when she'd said she was being picked up on time… She must have been up to something – maybe something like **sabotaging** our experiment!

"Aunty, I'm so sorry, but I'll have to help with those decorations later. I need to go and check something," I say quickly.

"Was it something I said?" Bindi jokes as I race past her down the stairs.

"Just going to Milo's, won't be long," I shout over my shoulder.

"It's 5.25 already! Be quick, **beta**, dinner is almost ready!" Granny shouts after me.

Milo is sitting down to his tea when I get to his house. His mum doesn't seem to be as upset as she was about the **foam flood** and offers for me to join him, but Milo is eating plain pasta with cheese and beans, which looks a bit **weird**, so I say, "No thank you," as politely as I can.

"Are you sure you don't want any, Neesh, it's **so yummy**!" Milo says as he shovels in another mouthful. His mum goes to the kitchen to get him some more juice.

"No, it's okay, Milo. I came over because I think I found another clue. Well, Aunty Bindi told me something that **I think** is a clue."

Milo stops eating. "What is it then? Don't tell me

– it was Mr Graft. It was, wasn't it? He was secretly trying to **drown** the school in foam so he wouldn't have to deal with us '**cretins**' any more, or whatever he calls us. What is a **cretin** anyway?"

"No, Milo, it wasn't Mr Graft. How do you come up with these **wild theories**? Listen, Aunty Bindi said that when she picked the twins up from school on Thursday to take them to the dentist, Beena Bhatt was still there in the playground too, hanging around with a big case in her hands." I sit back and let this new clue sink into Milo's thoughts. I wait for him to say something, but he just looks **puzzled**.

"You understand what this means, don't you, Milo?" I lean forward again.

"Um, that Beena needs a new backpack?"

"**No, Milo!**" I shout, waving my arms around. "It means Beena didn't get picked up by her driver when she said she was going to be. She was still at school when the **foam-plosion** happened, which means she had the opportunity to **sneak** into the **lab**. And she definitely has a motive – she **hates** me! Remember, she always goes out of her way to humiliate me. This would be her perfect **prank**."

"Ah, I get it!" exclaims Milo. "So we know the '**when**' and the '**why**', we just need to work out the '**how**'!"

"**Exactly!** …Wait a minute, have you been watching more of those detective shows? That all made a lot of sense!"

"Well, you know, I may have watched a few episodes of **Poirot** and some other crime mystery series. One was about a detective rat! You'll have to watch it with me some time – Ralph **loves** it." Milo beams.

"Okay," I laugh. "So it's agreed – tomorrow we investigate Beena Bhatt!"

HECTOR POI-RAT in
"THE MYSTERY OF THE
BLUE CHEESE"

CHAPTER ELEVEN

BEENA'S SECRET

The next morning, as we walk through the school gates, Beena Bhatt **flounces** up behind us and pushes past.

"Excuse **you**," she snaps as she heads through the gate before us.

"Did you notice?" I whisper to Milo.

"What, that she's **rude**? Yes, I definitely noticed that."

"No, not that. She always makes such a big show of having a **driver** to take her wherever she wants, but I didn't see a car pull up just then, did you?" I say. "Actually I don't think I've **ever** seen it! I only know she has a driver because she goes on about it.

In fact, I think she only started talking about having a driver after the twins moved to our school! What if she made it up to impress them? No one would ever challenge her or say she's lying, because everyone is too afraid of her!"

"You're right, that's **weird**," Milo says. "We need to watch her today – she might give something away."

I look around the playground and wonder again who else could be a **suspect**. I spot Mindy in her trademark scarf, her hair covering half her face as usual as she scowls at someone. Who is that? I move to see properly and realize who it is. It's **Govi** – our friend Govi. Since when did he talk to either of the twins? I grab Milo and walk over.

"Hi, Govi," I interrupt. Govi looks up, startled. Mindy steps back defensively and knocks into him, making him drop the pile of booklets he was carrying. She doesn't even stop to help or apologize. She just walks off. She's so **weird**...**and rude**!

"Where have you been, Govi? We were worried about you yesterday," I say as I bend to pick some of the booklets off the floor.

"I, um, was **ill** and I've been in trouble with Mum and Dad for being involved with the **foam flood**. Even though I told them it was an accident!" he adds quickly.

"What's with all the booklets, man?" Milo asks. "Even you can't read all these!"

"When my parents met with Mr Graft they asked him to keep me away from you guys, so he arranged for me to help out one of the teachers at break times.

136

I tried to tell them it wasn't your **fault**, but they just won't listen," he says sadly.

"That's so **unfair**," moans Milo, but I nudge him to be quiet. It's not Govi's fault all this happened.

"I don't think I've ever seen you talk to the twins before," I say, trying to change the subject, but also wondering **what on earth** Govi and the twins could have to discuss.

"Oh, well, you know, they asked me for some help with their maths homework, so, like, umm, well, I guess they're okay with me now? They're not so bad once you get to know them. Anyway, I'd better get these papers to the staffroom. See you guys later?"

"Just be careful. You can't **trust** them!" I call after him, but he's already disappeared around the corner with his huge pile of booklets.

Milo raises his eyebrows at me. "Well, that was weird!"

"Yup, definitely. But you know he just wants to

be liked. I do worry about him. I don't want those twins taking **advantage** of him."

I spend the rest of the day worrying. Something is bugging me but I'm not sure what. Usually I would be listening to the teacher in every lesson, but today, while the teacher talks about maths equations, I doodle in the back of my notebook: **names**, **clues**, a **timeline** of the day of the **foam explosion**. It swims about in front of my eyes. There's something I'm missing.

3.20 - School finishes
3.30 - Miss Bunsen leaves us...
3.33 - Loud bang!
3.35 - Foam everywhere!!!

At home time we **race** outside to try and catch a glimpse of Beena and her **mystery driver** before she leaves. The playground is full of parents and kids and at first I think we've already missed her. Then I catch sight of that bright pink jacket with the fur collar. No one else in our school has one like it. I grab Milo's arm. "Quick, Milo, look, there she is."

Milo pulls his hood up. "Come on then, let's follow her. We'd better try to blend in though – you know, **incognito**."

"Milo, it's a playground full of kids, I don't think we could blend in any more if we tried. Although your hair does make you stand out, so yeah, maybe keep the hood up."

We make our way across the playground, weaving through the crowd of kids trying to get out of the school gates. Beena gets there before us and turns left. Through the railings, I see her walking along. She keeps looking **left** and **right** and **behind**, as if she's worried someone might be

following her. Which, of course, we are, but we don't want her to know that.

"Better keep a safe distance, she seems on edge about something," I say.

We slip out of the gates and round past the railings, following her away from school and across the road. Beena turns down a dead end – one of those cul-de-sacs where there are just a few houses. She stops by a car, but it's not what I expected at all.

"That's her driver?" Milo **gawps.**

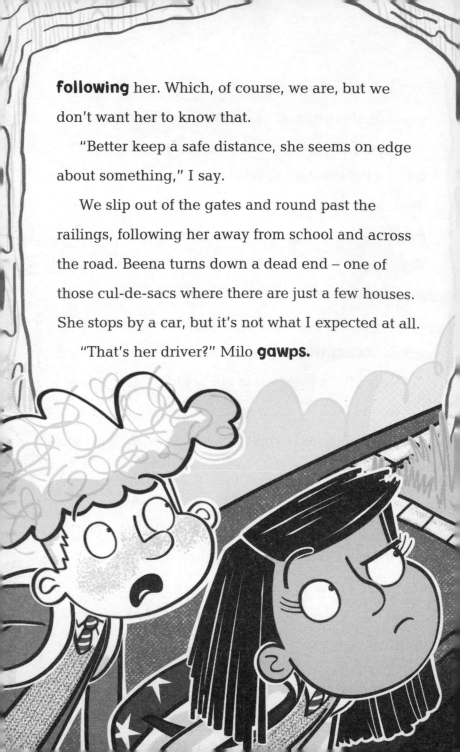

I know what he means. The car Beena has walked up to is gleaming white, with blue lights glowing underneath it and a thing stuck to the boot which looks like the wing from an aeroplane – I think it's called a spoiler. The registration plate says **PAV1**.

·PAV 1·

Just then Beena turns and spots us. She glares and stomps over, **scowling**.

"I don't know what you **think** you've seen, but if you tell anyone **anything**, there'll be trouble."

"I, erm, we just wanted to check you were okay," I **lie**.

"I'm fine, why wouldn't I be?"

Milo joins in. "Well you said you have a driver and that car is a little **unusual**, so we were worried you were getting in the wrong car or something!"

"What? **NO**!"

"Who is it then?" Milo tries to peer round her, but Beena stands firmly in the way.

"None of your business."

But then a voice calls out from the **gleaming** white car. "Ah, **Beena beta**, we should get going, your mother will be wondering where you've got to."

Beena's face is **very** pale suddenly and she quickly turns to answer, "Be there in a second, uncle." She swings back to us. "Like I said, if you tell **anyone** about this, **BIG** trouble!"

"So, let me get this straight, you **don't** have a driver?" I ask.

"Oh god, you're not going to let this go, are you? Okay, no, I don't have a driver, **as such**. I just said that because it's less **embarrassing** than my uncle and his **Pavmobile**." Beena rolls her eyes.

Milo snorts and says, "What's a **Pavmobile**?" just as Beena's uncle gets out of the car and comes to stand next to her.

"I'm Pav, **innit**. Beena's favourite uncle, eh, **beta**?"

Beena's eyes dart from side to side, making sure no other kids from our school are around. Then she turns to her uncle. "Yes, uncle. Now, come on, let's go – **quickly quickly**."

"Oh, Beena, just one more thing?" I call out.

"**WHAT** is it?" she snaps.

"My aunty said she saw you with a large case on Thursday. It wasn't anything to do with what happened in the science lab, was it?"

"What? **NO**! Now go away!"

"This case?" Beena's Uncle Pav pulls a black case from the back seat of his car.

"Ooh, yes, could I just...?" I say, and Milo and I dart over to the car and take the case from Uncle Pav before Beena can stop us, placing it on the floor.

"Please don't do that," Beena begs.

I ignore her and open it anyway. The lid creaks as I lift it. I'm half expecting to see potions and science equipment – but what I find is even more **shocking**. I close the case and re-open it in case the contents **magically** change. This can't be right! When I look up at Beena, she's gone a funny pink colour, almost the same shade as her coat!

"A **trumpet**?"

"Why has she got a **trumpet**?" Milo asks.

"A **trumpet**?" I ask again, really not believing what I'm seeing.

"Yes, a **trumpet**. Beena is getting very good, you know!" Uncle Pav tells us **proudly**.

Beena stomps over and gathers up the shiny trumpet. "Yes, okay, I go to trumpet practice every Thursday after school. **Happy now**?"
She pouts.

Suddenly I feel a bit sorry for Beena. She's still **awful** and **mean**, but she has relatives who embarrass her just like I do and she likes playing the trumpet. She's not so **super-cool** after all – at least, not in the way she wants everyone to think, anyway.

"I think it's pretty **cool** learning an instrument," I offer, "and we won't tell anyone if you don't want us to, right, Milo?"

"Um, no. I don't think anyone would believe us!" Milo shrugs.

"Thanks," she replies, almost nicely, packing her trumpet away. It's a **weird moment** and for a second no one knows what to say or do.

"We, er, we kind of thought you were involved in the **foam-plosion** at school," I admit.

"Duh, like I'd go to all that trouble! I do have a life, you know. Why would I care about some **dumb** science competition? I've got better things to do!" And just like that, Beena is back to being Beena and off she goes, plonking herself in her uncle's car.

"That's true," I say to Milo. Beena doesn't care about science. She doesn't like me, but she wouldn't know how to rig a foam volcano experiment and I doubt she'd bother trying to find out how. So that means we're back to **square one** again. We're still excluded from the science fair and **time is running out** to clear our names and get back in.

I think about this all the way home, while Milo talks about how he always wanted to learn to play an instrument and that he might take up the drums. I think about it through dinner, while Granny piles chapatis and vegetable curry on my plate, Mum natters on about her yoga class and Dad talks about his big important meeting. I think about it some more while I brush my teeth and even once I'm lying in bed…until eventually my brain gives up and I fall asleep. And then I dream about **giant foam volcanoes** chasing me and **trumpets blaring** while I climb one of Granny's colossal **leaning towers of chapatis** to get away.

CHAPTER TWELVE

FINDING THE TRUTH

The next morning at school, Milo and I try to work on our list of suspects.

☆ **Adil Ansa – has an alibi – was rehearsing for performance**

✳ **Beena Bhatt – was playing the trumpet!**

✩ **Mindy and Manny – at the dentist**

Who else is there? It's **hopeless** – we've run out of clues and out of time. The science fair is in two days and we still can't prove that the accident was a **set-up**. Milo and I sit in unhappy silence.

"What do the detectives do in those shows you watch, Milo?" I ask distractedly.

"Well, I guess they always return to the scene of the crime, but we already did that."

"Ah, but we didn't retrace our steps!" I realize.

"What, like **moonwalk backwards** through the lab and do everything in reverse, like we're on **rewind**?"

"Kind of, but maybe not **backwards**," I say with a smile.

"But when? The lab has classes in it this afternoon and we need to get in there as soon as poss, don't we?"

"Yes, which is why we're going to stay after school has finished," I decide.

"We can't afford to get in any more trouble, Neesh. We're banned from doing our project for the science fair, so how are we going to explain being in the lab if anyone sees us?"

I think for a minute. Milo does have a **point**.

I look around for inspiration and my gaze falls on Milo's backpack. Then just like that, I've got it — we need a **diversion**!

"Why have you got that **weird** smile on your face, Neesh? You're scaring me now!"

"Well, I've got a plan but it's a bit dangerous and it needs someone very brave," I begin.

"**Okaaay**, what do you need me to do?" Milo sighs.

"Um, well I wasn't thinking of you, Milo, I had someone much smaller in mind."

"That's a bit **rude**, Neesh, I don't think it's nice to comment on someone's size!"

I laugh then. "No, Milo, I'm talking about Ralph!"

"Ralph? What could **Ralph** do to help us? That Veena made a right **fuss** when she met him."

"Exactly!" I smile.

"I still don't get it. I've got a feeling this could be dangerous for my Ralphie," Milo said worriedly.

"I promise no harm will come to Ralph," I assure

him – although I'm not exactly clear on how or **IF** my plan will work.

At exactly **3.21 p.m.** as everyone else is leaving the classrooms and piling out of the playground, Milo and I hang back in a corner of the cloakroom, waiting for the building to clear.

Mr Graft's voice echoes from his office down the corridor. He must be on the phone. Mrs Bucket, the cleaner, has the vacuum out already and is working her way down the other end of the hallway. This is our **chance**.

"Are you ready?" I ask Milo.

"I don't know about this, Neesh."

"It'll be okay, Milo, I **promise** – it's the only way this will work," I insist.

"Okay, well, I'm trusting you."

"Thank you," I say, taking Milo's backpack from him gently.

Slowly
and
carefully
I lay the bag
on its side
and open the
zip. Ralph the rat
is **half-asleep** and
blinks his eyes at us a few times
before stretching his paws and looking around.

"Come on, little man, I've got **raisins**," I whisper
and I throw a few down the corridor.

The rat sniffs and closes his eyes again.

"Come on, Ralph, we **really** need your help,"
I plead.

"Let me try." Milo smiles as he gently lifts Ralph
out of the makeshift cage. Ralph stretches and looks
up at Milo curiously. Then the strangest thing
happens – Milo brings Ralph up to his face and **rubs
noses** with him. "We've got this, Ralphie.

Remember when I was training you the other night and you followed the **trail of treats** to get from one end of the maze to the other? It's just like that. Shall we try?"

Milo lowers his hand to the floor. Ralph scurries off, eating raisins and heading for the sound of the vacuum cleaner.

I lean in and murmur, "He really does understand you, doesn't he?"

Milo shrugs. "He said he doesn't mind helping, but can we please not let him get caught?"

I shake my head in **wonder**. Maybe Milo is an **animal whisperer** after all! We watch Ralph run down the hallway towards Mrs Bucket the cleaner. She's got her back to us. She'll never see him! Milo throws a few more raisins, which land in front of

Mrs Bucket's cleaning trolley. Ralph sniffs his way round the trolley and **straight** into Mrs Bucket's path. It takes a second for her to notice him, but suddenly, as she's hoovering, she comes face-to-face with **Ralph the rat**.

"AAAAARRRGGGHHHHHHHHH!"

Milo and I cover our ears. Mrs Bucket **shrieks** her way down the hall past us towards the head's office. Milo quickly runs over to the trolley and retrieves Ralph, putting his rat safely in his pocket.

"Well done, little fella," he whispers and feeds Ralph a little treat.

We hide back in the cloakroom as Mr Graft comes out of his office.

"What on earth? Mrs Bucket! Why are you screaming, is there a **fire**?"

"No, Mr Graft, worse than a fire. I saw a **RAT**!"

"Don't be ridiculous, why do people keep talking about **rats**? We've never had rats in my school, it's impossible!"

"I'm telling you, I saw a **RAT**!"

"Calm down, Mrs Bucket. There must be another explanation. Perhaps it was something else? A mucky old rag, a bit of dust?"

"Calm down? **Calm down?** I will not **CALM DOWN**! I'm not going back in there till you've dealt with that rodent problem. Get the **exterminators** in, do whatever needs doing. I will not be doing any more cleaning until it's sorted." Mrs Bucket folds her arms and stares **defiantly** at Mr Graft.

Mr Graft sighs. "Alright, Mrs Bucket, let's make our way outside and I'll call the caretaker from my mobile. He can put the traps out. I'll just make sure all the teachers have gone home first."

Milo grabs my arm. "Traps? We can't let Ralph get caught in a **TRAP**!"

"Don't worry, we've got him, remember! Let's hide in a classroom until everyone gets out and then we can do what we came here for," I whisper.

We wait for the noise of the last few teachers leaving to die down and soon the school is quiet. I'm guessing we don't have long, so we'd better be quick.

Milo and I walk down to the science lab, which is pretty much back to normal now after the **foam flood**. Our volcano still sits in a **soggy pile** in the corner of the room as a reminder to everyone of what happened.

My tummy **turns** when
I look at it.

"So what are we
looking for? We already
went through the volcano
and found nothing but one
of Govi's stickers."

"That's true. Whoever did this must
have known I would want to **investigate**, so they
covered their tracks well. Let's think **logically**.
So, we had measured everything out, we were just
getting the bicarb ready and we heard the noise
coming from the corridor."

"Right, so we went to look and it was Miss
Bunsen stuck in the cupboard."

"Okay, so in the time that we were out there,
someone could have been in the lab **pouring
bicarb** in the volcano to make it **explode**. And at
the same time, or shortly after, that person or
someone else made the **sprinklers** come on, so that

the foam **spilled** onto the floor and out along the corridor. And all of that from when Mrs Bunsen left the room up until we saw the foam **flooding** everywhere took how long? About 3 or 4 minutes, right?" I reason.

"How did they make the sprinklers come on, though, and would that really make so much foam?" Milo asks.

I think carefully. Why would the sprinklers come on? I guess usually sprinklers come on where there is a fire...or maybe when the system **THINKS** that there's a fire. "Milo, how would someone trick the fire safety system into thinking there was a fire? They would have had to burn something, right?" Then it comes to me: "I remember smelling **burned toast** right before the flood and wondering who would be making toast then? That might be it!"

"Should we go and look at the kitchen, Neesh?"

"Let's time ourselves. You be us in the lab and in the hallway. I'll go and hide in the kitchen. I think the cleaner left the door propped open so I just have to remember not to move the bucket! I'll pretend to pop some bread in the toaster and set it to high on the dial. Then I'll run back here to the lab through the other door, pretend to pour the bicarb into the volcano and then run back out to the kitchen to hide and let's see how long that takes. When I'm done I'll whistle so you know to stop the timer."

Milo gives me that look he usually gives me when he thinks I've **lost the plot**, but he does as I've asked anyway.

"Okay, timers ready – three, two, one, **GO**!"

I run out of the lab door and down the corridor to the staff kitchen. The door's open, as I thought. I do the actions of putting some bread in the toaster so we're accurate on the timing. But as I'm pretending, I knock a spoon off the counter and onto the floor. I think I'd better pick it up, but as I bend to get it

I bang my head on the edge of the counter and have to sit down. **Ouch, that really hurts.** Then I spot **IT**. Just lying on the floor, poking out from under the cupboard.

"Neesh, you can come out now!" Milo's voice approaches.

It looks like it's been shoved under there in a hurry. I pick it up. An empty carton of **bicarbonate of soda**. The thing that makes **foam**, the thing that caused all the **trouble**. So that's how the foam spread so quickly. It's starting to make sense now. Now we know **WHY** there was so much foam – someone used a whole carton of bicarb!

It's then that I see something shiny pushed further under the cupboard. I reach across and slide it out. It's a badge.

A special badge that only one person I know owns. A badge that says **Geology Rocks**.

Govi's badge.

My friend **Govi**.

Why would Govi's badge be here, in the staff kitchen where kids aren't allowed? When would he have been in here and why?

I try to push away the idea that is forming in my head. But it gets **stronger** and **STRONGER**. There was only one other kid around when the explosion happened. And he wasn't with us when we heard the noise and left the lab. He wasn't with us when I smelled the burning or when the sprinklers came on. He turned up when the foam was already overflowing.

GOVI.

CHAPTER THIRTEEN
THE LEANING TOWER OF CHAPATIS

GOVI.

How could he? And why? None of it makes any **sense**.

"Neesh, didn't you hear me calling? Are you okay, why are you on the floor?" Milo walks in and reaches out his hand to pull me up. "Neesh, what's wrong? Oh, is that Govi's badge? He'll be glad you found it, won't he!" Milo smiles, totally not understanding what this means.

I sit down on a nearby stool.

Milo shakes his head as I tell him what I think happened. "It can't be Govi, he's our **friend**.

Why would he do that? There could be another reason why he was in the kitchen."

"I almost can't believe it myself, but there's **no other explanation**, Milo. No one else was around that afternoon, and how else did the badge get here? Kids aren't allowed in this kitchen, it's for the teachers. He would have no reason to be sitting under the counter in here unless he was hiding." I take a second to collect my thoughts. "Think about it, Milo, Govi never wanted to make a volcano. **In fact**, he tried to leave the team at lunch last Thursday. I don't know, maybe he thought his only way out was to **ruin the project**!"

Milo raises his eyebrows. "That seems a bit **extreme**, Neesh. But possible, I guess. He is a little strange sometimes – even more than me!"

"Okay, so we agree it could have been Govi. So what if he told us he was going to get Miss Bunsen, but instead he shut her in the supplies cupboard. He ran to the kitchen and put a piece of bread in the

toaster on high so it would
burn and set the sprinklers off.
Then he could have run back
round to the lab through the other
door and waited for us to go out and investigate
the noise. While that was happening, he poured the

bicarb into the volcano to make
it froth, but that wasn't
enough to make a flood, so in
the meantime he **ran back** out
the side door and sprinkled
bicarb in the corridor
underneath the sprinklers.
When the sprinkler system
kicked in, the water and the bicarb did their job.
Even without vinegar the foam **flooded** the
corridor, joining the foam coming out of the lab."
I'm **breathless** by the time I stop talking.

Milo speaks slowly. "I guess it could be true, but
what do we do now? Do we just **confront** him? He

might cry! I don't want to make anyone **cry**. Should we tell a teacher? He could get in **big trouble**. He's still our **friend**, Neesh. There's got to be a reason why he would do something like this, knowing how much trouble we would get in."

"I know," I say, my mind **whirling**. The idea that Govi is the reason I can't take part in the science fair, the reason why the teachers don't trust me any more, just doesn't make **sense**, and yet the evidence is clear. What do I do when the clues point to Govi but my instinct tells me he couldn't be responsible?

We take the badge and the empty carton back to the lab and find a plastic ziplock bag to put them in. Then Milo and I walk home in a daze. **It's too awful.** I'm used to the twins being mean and Beena being **horrible**, but my own friend deliberately **sabotaging** us? My brain spins. We agree we'll confront Govi together tomorrow and give him the chance to explain before telling Mr Graft what we've discovered.

When I reach my house I pause outside the front door. I can hear chattering and music, and the smell of cooking wafts out into the street. Granny's big birthday party is on Saturday, the day after the science fair, and apparently there's still a lot to do. Though I walk into the house feeling really **sad**, I don't have much chance to feel sorry for myself, because as usual there is **chaos**. Oh no, Mindy and Manny are here, **in my house**! Aunty Bindi is circling round and round the living room, talking to someone called Bally on the phone. From what I can gather, there's a problem with the birthday cake Aunty Bindi ordered and she wants it sorted out **NOW**! Family occasions really bring out the **bossy** in her!

With a sigh, I start to walk upstairs, and run into Mum at the top.

"Hi, **beta**, how was your day?" she asks me brightly, as though it's not **the end of the world** downstairs.

"Okay, I guess," I lie. Mum means well and I know

she cares, but it's not even worth telling her the truth about my day, as she'd never believe it. I'm not sure I do.

"Well, I'm not convinced, your **aura** looks a bit off to me. Go and get changed and come back down for dinner. I'll go and calm Bindi. I don't know why she insisted on such a fancy cake. The supermarket has a beautiful selection for a fraction of the cost. They even make an organic, egg-free, sugar-free, fat-free flan!"

"That sounds…um…**yuck**!" I half-smile.

"Hmm, yes, I suppose it does." Mum smiles too and strokes my hair. "Are you sure you're okay, **beta**? I know all this business with the experiment and the school has been upsetting, but there will be other science fairs."

"I know, but this was **important** to me, Mum. It's my last year in junior school and now all anyone will remember about me is that I flooded the school with **foam**!"

"Well, look on the **bright** side. There's worse things to be remembered for!" Mum nudges me playfully and goes downstairs. She's trying to cheer me up, I know, but the thought of my friend Govi **deliberately sabotaging** something we'd worked on for so long is really hard to take.

"Oh, Anni, don't forget your cousins are staying for dinner today," Mum calls back. "Uncle Tony has to work late on his accounts, so Aunty Bindi asked if we could all eat together here. And we didn't get to see them last week with everything that happened, so it will be nice to catch up with them."

Great, I think, **just what I need, those two in my face with their snarky comments**. I go to my room and plonk my stuff down. I get my notepad out

and rip out the suspect list. I flip over to a new page
and write:

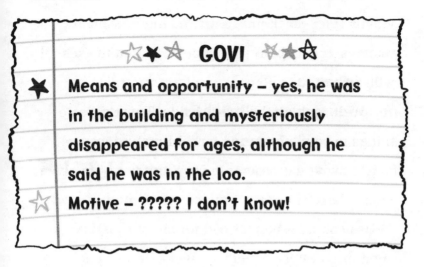

☆✦☆ **GOVI** ✦★✩

✦ **Means and opportunity – yes, he was
in the building and mysteriously
disappeared for ages, although he
said he was in the loo.**

✩ **Motive – ????? I don't know!**

I throw the notepad on my bed and get changed
into some comfy leggings and my favourite hoodie.

"Time for dinner, Anni. Come down, **beta**,"
Granny calls up.

I reluctantly go downstairs and notice the big
dining table has been pulled out of the garage and
plonked in the middle of the living room. Pretty
much the whole surface of the table is covered with
trays and plates piled high with food. Granny has

made her famous lamb curry, alongside an enormous **leaning tower of chapatis** – my favourite. There's Mum's spicy chicken drumsticks and seasoned potatoes, light, spongy chickpea and lentil cakes called **dhokra**, colourful and crunchy fried **poppadum curls** (which are like spicy crisps) and a big bowl of steaming rice. I make a mental note to avoid the vegetable dish, **saag**. **EURGHH**. Saag is basically spicy spinach and I don't care what they say about it being good for me, it's just the worst thing **ever**. If you've never eaten spinach, it's like cabbage but even **yuckier**. The grown-ups think it's delicious. They **MUST** have different taste buds to kids, that's all I can say.

There's literally no space to move around the outside of the table, so I have to **squeeze** myself along the edge of the room to get to a seat.

"Why aren't we just eating off our laps like normal or sitting on the floor?" I say, confused. I'm usually allowed to eat in my comfy chair.

Granny almost always sits on the floor to eat.
Suddenly we need the table?

"It was my idea actually, Anni, I thought it might be nice to eat round the table." Bindi smiles.

"She's all posh now that she's married to a businessman, eh?" Granny teases.

"No…" Aunty Bindi blushes. "But I thought it would be good for the twins to sit round the table with us. We are all a **big family** now, aren't we?"

I look over at the twins, who are sitting to the left of Aunty Bindi and looking just about as **uncomfortable** as me right now. Mindy is holding on to Bella, her dog, as though her life **depends** on it. Bella squirms out of her arms and jumps onto the sofa, curling up in a ball and promptly falling asleep.

"How's your dad, kids? I haven't had a chance to catch up with him recently." My dad smiles at the twins.

"He's okay, I guess, busy like always," Manny murmurs.

"Ah, well, that's to be expected. It's good he's **busy**, means the business is making money, and that's what pays for all your fancy gadgets and nice house and that poor bloke who chauffeurs you around. Malik, is it?"

"It's **Mustaf**," I interrupt, feeling embarrassed for the twins. Mindy looks up at me and then turns away really quickly.

Aunty Bindi takes a chapati from the **leaning**

tower Granny has made. She always makes too many, but that's Milo's lunch sorted for tomorrow – he'll be well happy. Aunty Bindi chews thoughtfully. "Anni, what is happening with your science fair project? Have they stopped all this nonsense about not letting you take part?"

I gulp and look from Mum to Dad to Granny next to me and even across at the twins. "Well, no. I'm still trying to figure out how the accident happened

in the first place and then maybe once I'm in the clear, they'll let me take part."

"And do you have a **suspect** in your sights?" Granny grins, nudging me.

"I'd rather not say," I mutter, giving Granny a **look**.

"Anni, **beta**, if someone else was responsible for that **foam flood** in the school, then you should tell the head teacher what you know! He was looking down his nose at me at the board meeting yesterday. I told him there must be another **explanation** for what happened, so if you have one, now's the time to share it!" Dad exclaims.

I can't help but smile at the thought of Dad sticking up for me. But even with that, there's no way I'm sharing what I know until I've spoken to Govi. The twins are looking at me with great interest now. **Is it hot in here?**

I concentrate on the leaning tower of chapatis. I'm quite particular about which ones I eat. It sounds **silly**, but I only like the ones which are perfectly round.

Luckily the one on the top of the pile is just that, so I stand on my tiptoes, lean over the table and try and pluck it away. Unfortunately when I pull the top chapati it seems to be stuck to the one below, which is also stuck to a few below that. So I tug it harder – maybe a bit too hard, as the leaning tower **wobbles** one way and then the other and then **collapses** across half of the table. Unfortunately, I also realize too late that while I was leaning over the table, the bottom of my **favourite hoodie** was dipping in the dish of **saag**. Yes, the **soggy** spicy spinach. **YEUCHH!**

"Are you okay, Anisha?" Mindy asks with a **smirk**.

"I'm fine," I splutter. "Just need to get this cleaned up." And I stagger off to the kitchen.

I turn the tap on and let the water run for a second. Granny comes in.

"Just getting some more **chapatis**," she tells me innocently.

"Don't **fib**, Granny, there's **loads** of chapatis. You can't miss them now I've **scattered** them all over the table!" I say.

"Ah, alright, I wanted to see if you were okay. What is going on, **beta**? You seem on edge."

"I'm okay... I just...well I found something out today about a friend. I found out that they **lied** to me, possibly **betrayed** me, and I'm just a bit **worried** about what to do," I say.

Granny looks at me for a moment, as if deciding on the best response. It's not often my granny is stuck for an answer.

"Well, I assume this is a good friend, otherwise you wouldn't be so worried. You know, if you feel this thing, whatever it is, is out of character, you should talk to your friend. Sometimes **good people do bad things** because they think they have no other choice. Or it could be they weren't the person you thought they were."

"That's what I'm **worried** about, Granny. You think you know who your friends are and who your **arch-enemies** are and that makes sense. But then if your friends do something that they know will hurt you, what are you supposed to do?"

"It definitely sounds like talking to your friend is the first thing, **beta**. Listen to Granny, okay?"

"Okay," I say uncertainly.

Before I can think any more about it there's some laughter from the living room, followed by Aunty Bindi's voice sounding indignant, so we go back to see what the fuss is about. Aunty Bindi is holding up what I guess is supposed to be a biscuit. Except it's all puffy and not like a biscuit at all.

"They were **supposed** to be cookies – I baked

them specially. Why are they like this?"

"Did you use the right kind of flour, for a start?" Mum asks.

"Er, yes, I'm not **daft**. I followed the recipe to the letter. Mostly," Bindi replies.

"**Mostly?** What does that mean?" Granny asks as we go over to the table to have a closer look. The **thing** Aunty Bindi is holding in her hand does not look like something you'd want for pudding. It's not cookie-shaped and it's not cake-shaped either. I reach over to feel it. Actually, it's a bit **marshmallowy**!

Aunty Bindi looks a bit sheepish now. "Well, I had a bit of a nightmare with them. The recipe said I needed **bicarbonate of soda**. I only bought a new carton the other week and I looked **everywhere** but I couldn't find it. So anyway, I went to get some more from the shop, and then the book said one teaspoon of bicarbonate of soda, but it didn't seem like very much so I added a couple more teaspoons. Also, I couldn't find an actual teaspoon so I used a tablespoon instead. I didn't think it would matter!"

Mum looks puzzled. "Would a bit extra really make that much difference? I never measure my ingredients!"

Mindy snorts. "Duh, Aunty, if you add too much bicarb of soda, obviously it makes it **expand**!"

I nod in agreement, impressed that Mindy knows about the effects of bicarbonate of soda.

But wait, **how** does she know that? **Why** would she know that? We haven't covered it in class – that's why it was going to make such a great experiment for the science fair.

A thought pops into my head. It couldn't be,

could it? But Aunty Bindi just said her **brand-new tub of bicarbonate of soda went missing**…in the **same week** that my volcano exploded foam all over school.

I shake my head. No, we know it was Govi who sabotaged us.

But then what if he had help?

Gullible Govi
+
Terrible Twins
=
Catastrophic consequences!!

CHAPTER FOURTEEN

WHO DID IT AND HOW?

After dinner, Aunty Bindi insists on trying out **party games** with us all in the marquee she's had put up for Granny's super-sized birthday. She makes us play charades and there's a particularly long round where no one manages to guess that she is trying to act out the film **Jumanji**. Her impression of a hippo leaves a lot to be desired. And it's probably best not to mention Dad's impression of a gorilla for the movie **King Kong** either. Then someone suggests we play **Cluedo**. The twins complain, but after a while they really get into it. Mindy is very **competitive** and – not surprisingly – **very** good at **lying**. When the game is finished, I look at the clock, hoping they'll be leaving soon so I can get to working out their involvement in the **sabotage**. No such luck though.

"Ooh, I've got a great idea, kids, shall we make some of the decorations for Granny's party? I used to love doing crafts when I was younger. Come on, it'll be fun!" enthuses Aunty Bindi. Manny jumps up quite excited, but Mindy hangs back.

"Come on, **Mindy beta**, I've got really cool stuff – you might even have some fun!" Bindi smiles.

Mindy rolls her eyes but follows Aunty Bindi over to the very large pile of colourful bags and boxes that has been growing for a week now. Bindi pulls out a large roll of black paper, some plastic tubs and paintbrushes.

"Right, this is just the **coolest**. Anni, you especially will love this! Sit down, kids, let's spread out and make some space on the floor."

"Ooh, is it slime?" Manny asks excitedly as Aunty
Bindi opens one of the tubs.

"Eww, no, not slime – it's very special paint. Try
it," says Aunty Bindi. "The woman in the craft shop
said it's great for parties."

"It doesn't do anything," complains Mindy as she
slaps her loaded brush onto the paper. She's right,
it's just clear.

"Wait for it... Didi, will you get the light, please?" Bindi asks Mum. "We just have to hold up this special torch to the paper and **voila**!"

Mum switches the light off and Bindi holds the special torch to the paper. Suddenly we can see where Mindy painted on the paper. In the torchlight, the sloppy brushstroke glows a beautiful purple. **Awesome!**

"See, I told you it was **BRILLIANT**!" Bindi beams. "I've got some special lights to shine on the banner at the party and it's going to look **amazing**. Right, no more messing about now, I need a nice big banner with Granny's name on it. **CHOP-CHOP.**"

"I'll get some drinks for everyone," I volunteer, suddenly remembering I have a **mission** and need some thinking space away from the twins.

My plan immediately backfires as Mum asks for a cup of chai, Dad wants juice and the twins join in (just to be **annoying**, I think) by asking for hot chocolate. Granny must see the look on my face as she offers to help. As soon as we're in the kitchen, I turn to her.

"What is it, **beta**, you want some hot chocolate or warm milk too?"

"No, Granny, I need your help. I'm not sure, but I think the twins might have had something to do with the foam flood."

Granny frowns. "But wait, Bindi was at the dentist with them that day. How is it possible?"

"It's a long story, Granny, but I think they convinced someone else to do their **dirty work** for them. Milo and I are pretty sure that Govi was the one who actually **caused the flood** on the day, but it feels **weird** that he would come up with that himself for no reason. The twins were at the dentist, but they were **clever**. They got Govi to set off the **foam-plosion** for them to get me in trouble."

"Right, well, we sort this out right now then, **beta**. We go in there and tell Bindi what we've found out. She and Tony can sort those naughty twins out."

"I can't, Granny. I need to clear my name at school and me just **thinking** I know what really happened isn't enough. I need **proof** that no one can argue with. I need a **plan** to show that they are the ones responsible. If I confront them, they'll just deny it and say they were at the dentist at the time of the accident. And they can make an excuse that they needed the carton of bicarb for a project. **They'll get away with it,** you know they will. You said I have to stand up for myself and that's what I'm going to do. I'll get proof that even Uncle Tony can't ignore, the best way I know how – **using my brain**!"

"That's my girl!" Granny grins. She gives me a big hug, squeezing me tight. "Right, let's go back in there and I'll watch them carefully. I'll say you're feeling a bit **unwell** and need to go and lie down, so you can concentrate on coming up with a plan!"

When we open the door to the living room, it looks like they've given up on banner painting and...oh no, they've just got the **Monopoly** out. That always ends badly – Dad is the **worst** cheater!

"Right, shall we start?" Dad asks.

I tiptoe round everyone and head up the stairs as Granny whispers to Mum that I'm going to lie down. I pause at the top and listen to my family.

"I'll be the banker, shall I?" Dad offers.

"Er, no!" Bindi pipes up. "You always cheat!"

"I do not!" Dad huffs.

Bindi turns to Mum. "Come on, you know he does!"

"Well, maybe it would be nice for someone else to have a turn," Mum replies, very diplomatically. "How about you, Mindy?"

Mindy looks up from her phone. "Me? Oh no, that's okay, Aunty."

"No, no, come on, you'll stop these two arguing, so you'll be doing me a favour." Mum smiles.

"Oh, okay, I guess," Mindy says uncertainly.

I think to myself, **We almost sound like a normal family.** Why can't everyone just get along? I wish Mindy and Manny would stop seeing me as their **enemy**. We might actually have fun together. Maybe if I can uncover what went on with the **foam flood**, I can say that to them. But for now, I've got to come up with a plan.

CHAPTER FIFTEEN

THE PLAN

The next day is Thursday, the day before the science fair and my last chance to find out who caused the **foam-plosion**. This is going to take some **serious science skill** and a lot of **help** from my friends.

I gulp down my cereal and a glass of juice. Granny hugs me tight and wishes me luck. I'm going to need it! I leave the house and spot Milo waiting up the road for me.

"Hey, Neesh, how's it going?"

"Um, there's no quick answer to that, Milo – let's walk and talk," I say, handing him a foil package of Granny's warmed-up chapatis. I talk while Milo munches and listens. I've come up with a plan overnight, but before we put it into action I've arranged for us to meet up with the other people we need help from. As we approach our school gates, I start to look out for them. I don't see them straight away, but in my message I'd told them to stay a bit hidden. Then I see a **foot** poking out from behind the big tree by the corner near the gate. I tug Milo's sleeve as kids go past us into the school. We hang back and then **duck** behind the tree too. There, waiting for us, are Veena the vlogger girl and Adil Ansa, the library monitor. "Thanks for coming. I wasn't sure you would," I say.

"I'll help however I can. Does it involve a costume change?" Adil asks hopefully.

"You said in your message that there could be more to the **foam flood** story?" Veena jumps right in.

"Well, yes, but I need your help to prove it. Both of you," I say.

"Okaaay, what do you want us to do?" Adil asks eagerly.

Later, at lunchtime, Milo and I are sitting in the canteen at our usual table. I notice Govi is sitting with the twins. He glances over and sees me looking right back at him. I smile as **sweetly** as I can force myself to. His cheeks turn pink and he looks down at his sandwich. Mindy and Manny don't seem to notice. I decided last night not to confront Govi yet. He could tip the twins off that we suspect them.

"Look, there's Adil. I hope he can pull this off," I whisper.

"Shall I send Ralph over there to listen in?" Milo offers.

"Er, no, Milo, can you imagine if he gets **caught**? The school already has the exterminator company coming in next week. Ralph needs to stay well hidden all the time now."

We try not to look like we're watching as Adil walks awkwardly near to where Govi is sitting with the twins. He has his arms full of books and **accidentally-on-purpose** drops one right by them.

"Watch what you're doing!" Manny barks at him.

"S-s-sorry," Adil stutters. "I have to get these books to the hall right away. I'm helping set up a little library area for the science fair tomorrow. I don't suppose you could **help** me?"

"Er, you suppose right!" Mindy waves him away.

"What about you, Govi, could you give me a hand?" Adil smiles. "After all, you're taking part now, aren't you?"

"What? No, we were banned from doing it after the **foam flood**." Govi glances at Mindy and then looks at the floor.

"Yes, but I heard that Mr Graft changed his mind! You're back in!" Adil lies.

"WHAT?!" Mindy shouts and then realizes everyone in the canteen has stopped what they're doing to look at her. "What do you mean they're back in? They flooded the school with foam and they're **rewarding** her...I mean **them**?"

"I don't know what made Mr Graft change his mind, I just overheard two of the teachers talking. **Sorry.** I think Anisha and Milo are going to be setting up a new experiment in the hall today. Anyway, I'd better get these books over there. Miss Bunsen wants to get this done before school finishes." Adil walks away from them and glances over at Milo and me with a **half-smile** when he's sure Mindy, Manny and Govi can't see. After a second Manny gets up from their table to get a drink. Mindy leans in to Govi and tells him something which makes him frown and shake his head. She grabs his arm then and **grits** her teeth. Govi looks **scared** and I think about going over to help him, but then I remind myself that he betrayed us. He can't be **trusted**.

Milo and I finish our lunch and get up to leave the canteen. We deliberately walk past Mindy's table.

"Are you **coming**, Govi? I just got the news we can enter the science fair after all!" I say brightly.

"Um, yeah, I'll be there in a bit if that's okay. I just have to help Manny with his maths homework," Govi replies, looking at the floor the whole time he's talking to me.

"Okay, no problem. We're just going to get a few things ready before afternoon lessons start. Maybe see you in the hall after school? Miss Bunsen said we can stay back a bit to set up, as there won't be time in the morning."

Govi sneaks a glance at Mindy, who nods ever so slightly. **WOW**, she's really got him under her control. Manny is not paying attention as usual and instead is looking at his phone.

"Oh, **no**, I can't stay back today, I have a family thing. But I'm really happy for you – for us, I mean – that Mr Graft changed his mind," Govi blurts out, his eyes immediately darting to Mindy, who is **glaring** at him.

"Me too. You know, everyone deserves a **second chance**!" I say, crossing my fingers behind my back because we haven't been given one yet. Let's hope Mr Graft sees things our way after all this!

When we get to the hall, Miss Bunsen is busying about, trying to stick up a very large banner and somehow getting herself all caught up in it. Milo runs over to help her while I look around for a good spot. I think she's so **grateful** to have a helper she doesn't question why we're here in the first place. The hall is long and rectangle-shaped. Around the four edges of the room, sixty square desks have been placed in pairs – one pair for each school, I guess. Each pair of tables has a sign on it stating the school that is being represented. No one thought to remove one of the desks for our school after our team was **banned**, so there's a space for us next to Adil's ant farm experiment. I had been worried Miss Bunsen would replace us with one of the other teams from our year, but I think it was too late to submit a new project to the organizers, lucky for us.

Oh, great. Milo is in deep conversation with Adil – I bet he's going to want to learn how to speak "**ANT**" now!

Just as I'm getting a few things out of my bag, I feel someone watching me. I turn around and it's Mr Graft. He doesn't look happy to see me. I look over for help from Milo, but he's untangling Miss Bunsen from some bunting. Bunting at a science fair! Aunty Bindi would **love** all this!

"**Anisha Mistry**, what might you be up to? You don't have any reason to be here since I **banned you** from the **science fair**!"

"Um, well I don't, but I also kind of do, sir – I was hoping to have a word with you."

"And what might that word **be**?"

"Well I was hoping you'd reconsider letting me come along to the science fair tomorrow? I know you said I was banned because of the **foam flood incident**, but I've set something up that will show for certain who was behind it."

Mr Graft eyes me sceptically. "Really! And what would that be?"

I quickly explain my plan to him.

"I have to get some things set up today or it won't work. Please, sir, I really **can** prove it wasn't my fault that the volcano flooded the school with foam. Just give me the chance to show you? I've always been **trustworthy**, haven't I?"

Mr Graft looks at me, first sternly, then almost kindly. "Okay, **okay**, you have always been a good student, so I'm willing to give you the benefit of the doubt for now. The more I ponder on it, the more **baffling** it becomes. I'm not sure how it could have spread so quickly and it seemed to be coming from every direction at one point. Very strange indeed. Okay, you have my permission. Do what you need to, but I have to warn you, if any school property is damaged the consequences will be severe."

GULP. I'd better get this right then.

CHAPTER SIXTEEN

THE SCIENCE FAIR

After hardly sleeping, I wake up on Friday morning with **knots** in my stomach. When Milo and I eventually left the hall last night, our experiment was all set up: **volcano version two** (made in a hurry and not very sturdy), with the sachets of bicarbonate of soda next to it and all the other ingredients needed. I've got no idea what we're going to find when we go in today, but I hope it proves we are **innocent**.

When I go downstairs, Mum and Dad have already left for the day and Granny is making her special Indian **rice pudding**. Another one of my favourites!

"It's not ready, before you ask," she says as I try to

sneak up behind her. How did she know I was there?

"Oh, I suppose I'll have some later," I say, disappointed. "I'm not sure eating would help my **stomach** right now anyway."

"Shall I make you some home remedy? Always works!" Granny offers.

I think about the home remedy Granny makes with milk, funny-tasting seeds and salt. **BLEURGH!**

"Er, no thanks, I'll be okay. It's just **nerves** about today. We left everything in place last night before we came home."

"You'll be fine. This will put everything right, the school will see that you were not to blame for the **foamy flood** and you can get back to being a **science star**."

"I **hope** so, Granny. I'm just worried about what will happen if we find out **IT IS** the twins who were behind it. Why can't we all just get along?" I groan.

Granny chuckles. "Well, because you're family. I'm not saying the way the twins behave is okay, as they do take things **too** far. But, **beta**, they have come into a new family. They are still figuring out how they fit into all this. It's such a shame – I think you could all be really good friends if they would just trust you. Maybe this is the only way they know how to express their **frustration**."

"I don't know about that, Granny. Anyway, I'm going to be late. Wish me luck. I'm going to need it," I say, kissing her on the cheek.

Granny shakes her head. "Well, good luck, **beta**, I'm proud of you, remember that. And think about what I said!"

Milo and I meet at the end of the road and walk up to school. Milo tells me about Ralph's latest **escape** attempt. Apparently, last night he tried to get into the tank with Larry, the lobster Milo rescued from my Granny's cooking pot!

As funny as that sounds, I can't get my mind off what might happen today. I weigh up the probability of a good outcome, but that just makes my head **hurt**.

When we get to school, Govi is in the playground, sitting on a bench and looking a bit lost. We go over.

"Hi, Govi. Are you okay? You look a bit pale," I say. I'm not lying either – he looks **practically green** and his hands are **trembling** by his sides.

"I'm okay. Let's just get to the hall, the fair will be starting soon," he replies, quickly getting up from the bench and walking towards the main building. Milo and I look at each other. No going back now.

As we walk into the hall there are already a few of the other schools setting up. We wind our way through the crates and banners towards our table where we left everything ready yesterday. And then Milo spots it.

"Oh no, Neesh, our **volcano**, look!" Milo points.

Milo, Govi and I run over to our table. The cardboard volcano we had quickly put together is torn down the side, and there's some foam swilling about in a **mucky mess** in the middle of it.

"That's okay, Milo, really, it's **okay**," I say calmly, touching his shoulder and looking over at Govi.

Govi just stares at the floor. "I, um, I'll get some paper towels to clean it up. I...just...I'll be right back," he stutters and dashes off.

Miss Bunsen looks over and sees what's happened. She goes over to Mr Graft and whispers in his ear. **Our plan is in motion.**

At **10 a.m.** it's time for the official opening of the science fair. The **butterflies** in my tummy start **looping the loop** and I'm sure my face has gone a funny colour. I really hope we can pull this off – I don't know what will happen if we don't, but it won't be **good**. Mr Graft looks over at us and nods as he gets up onstage at the front of the hall. The room is bustling now, buzzing with excited kids and teachers. The tables set up around the edges of the hall are covered with **bubbling cylinders** and **vials**, **colourful steam** rising into the air along with a whole range of **weird** and **wonderful** smells. People are busy chatting and not paying attention to the stage at all, so Mr Graft does a little cough into the microphone, which vibrates round the room. Everyone turns to look at him.

"Ahem, right, **welcome,** everyone, to the, um, eleventh **National Schools Science Fair**!"

There's a ripple of applause and then silence, apart from a high-pitched **squeal** coming out of the speaker as Mr Graft stands too close to it with the microphone.

"Right, um, well without further ado I am delighted to introduce our host – a late change to the schedule, but a very welcome one. We have someone I know you'll all recognize from her very popular inter-web-net channel: **Veena Roop**!"

Then there's a proper round of applause and even

some cheering as Veena walks onto the stage.

"Hello, everyone! Teachers, students, welcome, as Mr Graft has already said, to the eleventh National Schools Science Fair. I understand that over one hundred schools applied to take part in today's competition and that has been narrowed down to just thirty. So well done to all those here today, you're already **winners** as far as I'm concerned! I'll talk a bit more as the morning goes

on, but for now I know the students are eager to show you all their hard work, so shall we just get on with it? Let's see some **spectacular** science!"

Everyone claps and then, just like that, the science fair starts. Students turn to their experiments and projects. Wheels and cogs start turning, water sprays, lights flicker – it's a real sight to see. All this science in our school hall! Despite everything, I smile, because it's so **awesome** to watch people

enjoying the stuff I like to learn about. Milo and I wander round some of the stalls to see what projects the other schools have made. Govi says he'll stay with our broken volcano. He looks **sad** but I don't question him.

There are so many **cool** experiments here. We walk past a boy holding a glass upside down with a marble spinning inside of it and the marble doesn't fall out! There are two girls with an amazing 3D model of the planet Saturn. Another table has Petri dishes with different types of bacteria, which is both gross **and** fascinating.

There's a bit of excitement when a **life-size** model of the human body gets knocked over on one of the stands and suddenly there are **papier mâché**

organs rolling about all over the floor. We run to help gather up the paper heart and lungs and a bit of crumpled brain. Luckily the two kids in charge of that stand manage to put their model back together, although it's a bit lopsided.

I check the time on my watch. It's **10.18** exactly. In twelve minutes it'll be time. I go to stand near our table and **what's left** of our volcano. Someone has placed a cone on the floor to keep people away from our stand. Milo hovers near the next table with Adil, talking to the ants in his ant farm. The hall is filling steadily and soon every stand has quite a few people

around it. Just then I see Mindy, Manny and Beena approaching us. Govi looks like he might **throw up** and mumbles something about needing the toilet. As he scuttles off, Mindy

squeals, "Oh dear, what happened to your experiment, Anisha? You really do have the **worst luck**, don't you? Maybe it's a sign to give up!"

"Actually," I say with a smile, "I've realized I can still make an interesting experiment out of this."

"Really? What's that then?" Manny asks.

"You'll have to wait and see," I say, turning my back on them, which I know will **infuriate** Beena. I hear them **stomp** away and turn around when I think it's safe. My watch now says **10.29**. It's almost time.

Veena comes over with the microphone dangling from her hand. "I have to thank you for suggesting I host today, I'm actually quite enjoying it! It's **great** for my media studies module too so my teacher was happy to let me come over! Charlie is around here somewhere with his video camera. Anyway, all ready?" She gives me an encouraging smile.

"I think so," I say. "I really hope this works."

"You're the **smartest kid** I've ever met. You've

got this," Veena replies and switches on her microphone.

"If I can have your **attention**, everyone, we've got some **exciting** demonstrations happening this morning and we're about to see the first one now. I'm going to choose some very **special** helpers first. Let's see, who have we got in the room?"

I see Govi has returned and is standing at the back of the hall. He shrinks a little as Veena scans the hall. Mindy and Manny stand bold, clearly not thinking she'll pick them. Someone at the back of the room shouts out, "I **love** you, Veena!"

"Ah, well, I **LIKE** you all very much too. Right, now let's see, who do I want to help me out here. Aha, yes, you – yes, **you** with the badges – come on, don't be shy now."

Govi looks **horrified** as Veena pulls him out of the crowd and plonks him by our stand.

"Now, who else? Yes, yes, let's have you two there – yes, that's right, I'm looking at **you**." Veena chuckles as the twins shuffle forward, also looking **mortified**.

Mr Graft stands to one side, watching the whole scene with interest, but says nothing.

"Right, so now we have our volunteers, I'll hand you over to our very **talented** junior scientist, Anisha Mistry!"

There is some scattered applause as Govi and the twins look **super confused**.

"Well, um, I was part of the project team so I guess you don't need me?" Govi says hopefully.

"From what I can see your volcano is **wrecked**, so I don't know what experiment you can do here," sniffs Mindy. Manny nods in agreement, but looks around as if someone in the crowd can **save** him.

"Hmm, yes, that's true. Our volcano experiment is wrecked. Funny that it wasn't wrecked yesterday evening and now it is. How do you think that could have happened?" I ask, starting to feel more **confident**.

"Well, how should **we** know? You don't have a good track record really, do you?" Mindy smirks.

"Do you mean the **foam flood**? The one that we both know wasn't my fault?" I say.

"What is she talking about, Mindy?" Manny looks at his sister, **confused**. Mindy ignores him.

"What are you trying to say, Anisha? Are you **accusing us** of something?" Mindy glares. "Because I don't think you have any **proof** to back that up."

"I'm so glad you brought up **proof**." I smile. The room around us is silent. I'm sure no one else in the room has the faintest idea what we're talking about, but they're all **hooked**, listening and waiting to see what's going to happen.

"Govi, Mindy and Manny, would you say you've never touched this volcano before? Govi, you said you couldn't stay yesterday because you had a family thing, so you went straight home after school, right?"

Govi **gulps**. "Yeah, right...I mean, yes, I went straight home."

"And you, Mindy and Manny, you had no reason to come anywhere near the hall before this morning, did you?" I ask.

"Umm, no, why would we?" Manny replies, looking more and more **uncertain** by the second. "Mindy, is there something I should know?" he asks quietly. I'm starting to wonder if he was in on it after all. He's gone very **pale**.

"Okay," I continue, "well, an **interesting** thing

about this second volcano we built is that I added a little feature that no one but Milo and I knew about. **UV paint**." I stop and let that fact settle in. I can tell that Mindy and Manny still don't get it, but a **look of realization** crosses Govi's face.

"**UV paint**," he repeats slowly.

"Yes. For anyone who doesn't know, UV paint is **very** clever. In normal light it's just clear, so you wouldn't see it. But under a very special light it shows up as purple. My Aunty Bindi has been using UV decorations for my granny's big birthday party. I realized yesterday that we could use it to **catch** the people responsible for **wrecking** our first volcano and **flooding** the school."

The hall is silent as I continue.

"Before we left yesterday evening, I painted a thick **gloopy** layer of Aunty Bindi's UV paint all over our volcano. I knew the person responsible for sabotaging us the first time wouldn't wait long to **ruin** this volcano too and we only told one group of people. They might have thought they had just touched some clear sticky stuff and either wiped or washed their hands to get it off. But the **funny** thing with paint is that there are usually **traces** of it left behind. Could someone flick the light switch please?" The lights go out and the room darkens. I pull out my UV torch and scan it across Govi, Manny and Mindy. There are **flecks** of purple on Govi's glasses and jumper sleeves and **spatters** on Mindy's cardigan. Weirdly, Manny is clean.

The room **gasps**. Someone flicks the lights back on. Mindy's face turns **red** and Manny takes a step backwards.

Manny stares at Mindy, mouth hanging open. Okay, so he **DIDN'T** know what was going on.

"You can't **prove** anything," Mindy says. "Even if you're right about this volcano, it doesn't mean we had anything to do with the **foam flood** last week."

I'm about to explain to Mindy and everyone else about all our other **evidence,** but then I notice Govi staring at his jumper for a second, smiling. "UV paint. So **simple** but one hundred per cent **effective**. I should have known you'd **outsmart** us."

"**Shut up!**" Mindy hisses, but Govi **ignores** her and continues.

"You're the **cleverest** person I know, Anisha. I don't know why I ever listened to Mindy. I'm so **sorry** to you and Milo. It all got out of hand really quickly. I just wanted people to **like** me and Mindy was so convincing, she said she could make that happen if I helped with her plan for the **foam flood**. I never thought you'd get in so much trouble."

"How could you not know **WE** already liked you, Govi? You didn't need to do that. I wish you'd **talked** to us. Milo and me, we would have had your back. We're your friends."

"I know, I realize that now! I was feeling **left out** because you and Milo have known each other for like **for ever**. I guess I also just got so caught up in wanting everyone else to accept me and I couldn't see how I could ever make that happen. It seems so **silly** now. Can you ever **forgive me**? I understand if you can't. But I promise, no more **secrets** from now on."

I think about it. I was so **hurt** when I realized Govi had sabotaged us, but now I can kind of see why he did it.

"It might take some **time** but we can try, can't we?" I say. "Why don't you come to my house this weekend? We're having a **party** for my granny's birthday tomorrow. Would your mum let you come?"

"I think I might be grounded for a long time – like **eternity** – but thanks for asking. It means a lot." Govi's eyes are watering and I know he's really, genuinely **sorry**.

Mr Graft comes over then. "Well, I think I owe you an apology, Miss Mistry. It seems you did **NOT** flood the school with foam after all."

"No, sir," I say quietly.

"Well, I've had a quick word with the judges and they are going to **allow** your UV detector experiment into the competition."

"Oh, thank you, sir!" I **squeak**.

"That's alright. Govi, I can't believe you would allow yourself to be involved in something like this."

Govi hangs his head. He's not used to being **in trouble**. I don't think he knows what to say.

Mr Graft notices Mindy lurking nearby. "Yes, young lady, you can come here as well. I really despair. I just don't know what to do with you. How could you **frame** an innocent person that way, not to mention cause such **damage** to school property? This is a serious **offence**."

"We were just playing a **trick**. I thought it would be funny to see **goody-two-shoes** Anisha in trouble for a change. She thinks she's so **perfect**. I just wanted to take her down a peg or two. I guess it went too far, maybe it was **wrong** to get Govi involved as well." Mindy **sulks**.

"I'm sure Mindy didn't think it would flood **half** the school. Maybe she got a bit carried away," Manny pipes up. Even now he defends her. I guess family is still family.

I'm shocked, though, that Mindy thinks I have a perfect life. **If only she knew!** Plus she admitted she was **wrong** to do what she did. Am I hearing this right?

Mr Graft looks at Govi and Mindy sternly. "Right, well I'll deal with you two later. Needless to say, we'll need to meet with your parents as soon as possible."

I think of how Uncle Tony and Aunty Bindi are going to react to all this. Govi's parents are probably going to be furious – **again**. He's normally a star student.

"Maybe it could wait till after the weekend?" I blurt out hopefully. "You see, it's our granny's seventy-fifth birthday tomorrow and it's a big family occasion. It would be a shame to spoil it with all this and I'm sure Mindy is **very sorry** and promises not to cause any more trouble?" I nod at Mindy encouragingly. She stares at me, **shocked**.

"Hmm, well I do have a date this evening... I could do without a late parent meeting. I'm learning salsa, you know!" Mr Graft sees our startled expressions and clears his throat. "Anyway, I'd say you're very lucky to have Anisha as your cousin, Mindy. I'll let it go for now. I will be calling your parents on Monday though, so I suggest you explain to them what's happened during a quiet moment over the weekend before I give them the official version. Now run along."

Mindy looks **relieved** and mutters a quiet, "**Thank you, sir**," to Mr Graft before scuttling off to the other side of the hall. Manny follows her, but from what I can tell, he's not **impressed** by what she's done.

Just as I'm about to have an **awkward** silence standing with Mr Graft, Veena's voice comes over the speakers. "Hello, everyone, I hope you are enjoying the science fair. After all that **excitement** please don't forget there are lots more demonstrations taking place for you all to see, but before that our judges have already been round this morning and I think they are ready to announce a **winner**."

The judges take their seats on the stage and the head judge passes an envelope to Veena. Milo comes to stand next to me. I know it's not going to be us, as there are so many **amazing** experiments here today. But it's okay – we found the truth and proved our **innocence**, which was the best outcome I could have asked for.

Veena opens the envelope slowly. She pulls out a card and reads it out loud, smiling broadly: "**And the winner of the National Schools Science Fair is...**"

There's **silence** as everyone holds their **breath**, waiting to hear the result. I look across at Mindy and Manny and they are both looking right back at me, sort of smiling! Mindy crosses her fingers and holds them up for me to see. Is she **actually** crossing her fingers **for me**? Manny does the same and smiles too. They actually **want** me to win now? This day is too confusing. Did I actually make a difference to Mindy? I didn't think it was possible! I'm so busy thinking all this over that I almost miss it when Veena says, **"...Anisha Mistry and Milo Moon for their UV detector experiment!"**

Milo looks at me and I look around in disbelief. People are **clapping** and **cheering**. Mindy and Manny are clapping! "Did we just **WIN**?" I ask Milo.

"Yes, Neesh, we actually **WON**. **You did it! WE ACTUALLY DID IT!**"

And suddenly we're **jumping** up and down and **smiling** and **laughing**, and it's the best feeling **EVER**.

The next day is **Saturday**, the day Aunty Bindi has been waiting for. The day my granny turns **seventy-five**. From the moment I wake up, the house is in **CHAOS**. Aunty Bindi stayed at our house and has been awake **all night**, putting up decorations and hanging fairy lights pretty much everywhere she can. I get dressed in a pair of leggings and a **churidar top** in a deep blue with silver embroidery, which I only agreed to wear because it kind of reminds me of the night sky and the stars.

I come down for breakfast to find Aunty Bindi putting extra bunting up. I think we have every type of party decoration you can imagine in the living room and the marquee – balloons and foil spirals hanging down from the ceiling, sparkly table confetti on every surface. There's a **giant** portrait of Granny when she was a girl on the wall. She looks so different. In the picture she's dressed in a judo uniform and posing in a high kick position. I never knew Granny was into that but it totally makes sense.

"I had the looks, yes?" Granny chuckles, sneaking up on me as she always does.

"Oh yes, you were very **cute**." I laugh, putting my arm round her. "**Happy birthday, Granny.**" And I kiss her on the head.

She throws her hands up and says, "Ah, thank you, **beta**, but don't be getting too soppy on me. I've already had Bindi sobbing at me this morning. She's been looking at old photos and getting all **emotional**. Anyone would think **she's** the one turning seventy-five!"

Mum glides past us wearing a green **churidar**

with a shimmering pink scarf and hugs Granny. "Happy birthday, Mum." Mum and Aunty Bindi's parents live back in India, so they don't see them very often. I think that's why they're so close to Dad's mum, my granny.

"Ah, all this **fuss**, there was no need, I kept telling Bindi," Granny protests.

"Now, now, you only turn seventy-five once!" Dad scolds as he comes over and hugs Granny. "**Happy birthday**, Mummy."

A few hours later, guests are arriving. The DJ has set up in the marquee and is playing some old Hindi songs. Aunty Bindi is fussing around Granny, who keeps waving her away. Mum is sitting on a chair at the back of the marquee by herself. I go over.

"Are you okay, Mum?"

"Yes, **beta**, all fine, just thinking."

"About what?"

"About our family and how **lucky** we are to have each other." Mum smiles. I look around the marquee. The decorations look **amazing**. The banner we made with Granny's name in UV colours is lit up by the special black light Aunty Bindi bought, and it makes me smile. Our whole family and quite a few people I haven't seen since the wedding are having a great time. Even Granny Jas, who **grumbled** so much about having a big party, seems to be enjoying herself. She put on her best silk saree for today, and Dad places a **crown** on her head that Aunty Bindi made from **foil card** and covered in **sparkly gems**. Granny laughs and tries to take it off, but Dad insists. I think Granny secretly is quite **pleased** with all the fuss, but she'd **never** admit it.

Just then, Mindy and Manny come over.

"Ah, hello, you two!" Mum smiles knowingly and gets up from her chair. "I guess you kids have some stuff to discuss, I'll leave you to it."

"Hi, Anisha," Mindy says.

"Hi," I reply, unsure what to say next.

"So, erm, that thing you did for me yesterday – you know, asking Mr Graft not to call Dad until Monday? You know, you didn't have to do that. I know I've been pretty **mean** to you – I set you up to **fail**. Why would you **help** me after all that?" Mindy asks.

I think for a second before I reply. "Well, I guess even with everything – I'm not saying I'm okay with it – but...we're **family**."

They both look **shocked**. Manny coughs a little and changes the subject, nodding at the room. "Um, it's a good party. Bit too **colourful** and **loud** for me, but your granny seems to be having **fun**."

"You know, she's kind of **your** granny too now,"
I say.

"Really? We only have Dad's mum and dad
as grandparents and they just sleep a lot and watch
those boring Indian dramas on telly," Manny
moans.

I smile. "Well, Granny always said she would
have liked more grandchildren. I'm sure if you get
to know her a bit better, you'll see how much fun
she is."

"Yeah, but we're not really her grandchildren,
are we? You're her actual granddaughter by blood.
Bindi's not our mum and we're just here because she
married our dad. So, we're not **really** family,"
Mindy replies matter-of-factly. Manny looks like
she's **punched** him in the stomach.

"Well," I say slowly, "family isn't always decided
by blood, you know. I know you didn't choose to
become part of this family, but you're here now. And
you can choose to get to know us. **Simple as that**."

"Simple as that?" Manny repeats.

"Yep," I say. "Now, I don't know what you two are doing, but I'm going to get some **marshmallows** from the **chocolate fountain** before your dad **eats** them all!" I nod over at Uncle Tony, who has piled a plate rather **high** with **gooey** chocolate-covered marshmallows.

"I'm coming!" Manny calls out.

"What about you, Mindy?" I say.

Mindy looks me up and down carefully. "Okay, **deal** – on one condition," she says.

"What?" I say, thinking she's going to suggest something that will be **bad** for my **health**.

"I get the biggest marshmallow!" she yelps and runs off ahead of us.

Manny and I look at each other and **laugh**, then run after her. Who knew Mindy could be **funny**? Turns out we can all **surprise** ourselves sometimes.

A bit later I find Bindi by the **cake**, putting all the candles on.

"Hi, Aunty. Looks like all your hard work **paid off**," I say.

"Ah yes, everyone is having a **nice time**, aren't they? Even those twins of ours!"

"Yeah, they're not so bad you know, Aunty."

"Really? **YOU'RE** saying they're not that bad! What's going on?" Aunty Bindi narrows her eyes at me.

"Nothing much. I'll let them fill you in, but basically I think it's going to be **okay** between us from now on," I say – and for once I actually do think that. I'm not saying the twins and I will be best friends or anything, but I think we have an **understanding**.

"Anyway, I wanted to say thank you, Aunty."

Aunty Bindi stops counting candles for a second and looks up. "What for, **sweetie**?"

"You know, for your advice the other day and just for listening to me, I guess." I shrug. Aunty Bindi smiles and I think I see a **tear** in her eye. "You know, Anni, I'm always here if you need me."

She pulls me into a **hug**. I wriggle but I squeeze back just a tiny bit.

Soon it's time to bring out Granny's cake, which is a **huge** three-tiered thing covered in **sparkly** sprinkles and a lot of **candles**. Granny has to stand on a chair to be able to blow them out! We sing "**Happy Birthday**" and she blows them all out in one go! Everyone **cheers**.

Then there are **fireworks** in the garden, big loud ones. Aunty Bindi has really gone all out with this party. The smell of burning fills the air. Milo turns up, looking a bit **dishevelled**.

"Are you **okay,** Milo? Where have you been?"

"I had a **slight** accident. **Ralph** was having some time out of his cage and I only looked away for a second but when I turned back, he'd gone off **exploring**! It took me ages to figure out where he'd gone. He'd only got himself **stuck** behind the fridge. I was quite worried but we managed to get him out. I've put his cage next to **Larry the lobster's** tank now. I think Larry likes it. I **swear** they talk to each other when I'm not there!"

I smile. Milo is a total **weirdo** sometimes, but in the best possible way.

Just then Bindi grabs the microphone from the DJ and announces, "Everyone, we have a very special **performance** for our beloved Granny Jas, the head and heart of our family. **Happy birthday, Granny.**"

Uncle Tony joins her at the front. The DJ starts a new song and I recognize it immediately. Aunty Bindi **loves** the old Hindi movies and this is from one she and Granny have watched together many times. The song is called "**Baar Baar Din**" and it's a birthday song. To my surprise, as Bindi takes the mic and sings along, Mindy and Manny come to the front too and start singing with her and Uncle Tony! Even Bella the dog joins in with her own **woofy** style of singing. Maybe they are starting to feel a little like a **family** after all.

As I'm watching everyone, Dad comes over, holding his phone up to me. "Look, Anni, it's the email for your **prize** from the science fair. The **space centre** you're going to visit, it's not where you'd think it would be."

"Oh, it's **not**? Well, where is it then?"

"That's the wonderful thing! It's in Leicester!"

"**LEICESTER?!**"

"Ooh, they have the **BEST** Indian shops in Leicester!" Mum exclaims.

"**Who's going to Leicester, I want to come!**" squeals Bindi as she comes over to see what we're talking about.

"I could stock up on my spices!" says Granny.

"And the National Forest isn't too far from there – they do **lovely** cabin retreats. It's **so** relaxing to be out in nature," Mum adds.

"I have that friend who owns a minibus company, I'm sure he'd do me a deal and you know what we haven't done in **ages**?" Dad asks, smiling.

I shake my head, but I have a **funny feeling** in my tummy and I think I know what's coming next.

Mum grins, Dad grins, Granny grins a big toothless grin and Bindi jumps in the air, squealing. Then all at once they shout,

"FAMILY ROAD TRIP!!!!!!"

My family
+
a minibus on the motorway
=
Holiday horror
+
send help!!!

RAT
FACT FILE*

Name of animal: Rat

Scientific name: Rattus

Facts:

1. Rats have excellent
   memories! In fact,
   once rats learn a navigation route,
   they won't ever forget it.

2. Rats chatter and make
   happy laughter sounds, so
   Milo always knows when
   Ralph's in a good mood.

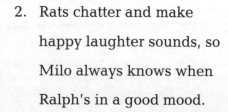

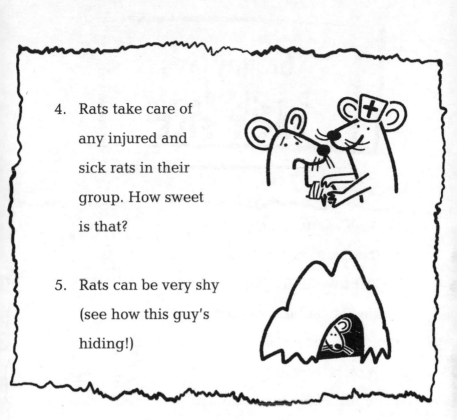

4. Rats take care of any injured and sick rats in their group. How sweet is that?

5. Rats can be very shy (see how this guy's hiding!)

★☆☆☆✫★✾☆★★✿✾★☆☆★✫☆★★✾☆✾★✿★☆✾★☆✫★✿☆✫

* Milo asked me if I could add in these fun facts about rats which he's been collecting for his special animal fact file. It's funny really, as I never thought rats were very cute until I met Ralph, and now I think they get kind of a raw deal. I mean, look at these facts! They sound like the animal kingdom's good guys.

Granny Jas's Paratha Recipe

You will need:

- A grown-up to help
- 2 cups of chapati flour*
- 1 cup of tightly packed methi (fenugreek) leaves, finely chopped*

- 1 teaspoon of turmeric
- A pinch of salt
- A pinch of ground paprika
- 2 cloves of garlic, finely chopped or ground into a paste
- 3-4 tablespoons of extra virgin olive oil
- 150ml of hot water
- Spray cooking oil

- 2-3 tablespoons of butter

* This can be found in the World or International Foods aisle of big supermarkets. However, if you get stuck, you can use one cup of wholemeal flour and one cup of plain white flour.

※ Place the chapati flour,
the methi leaves, turmeric,
salt, paprika, garlic and
extra virgin olive oil into
a large bowl.

✽ Ask your grown-up to add
the hot water slowly, mixing
with a wooden spoon to form
a dough.

☆ Scatter some chapati flour onto a flat service.

★ Divide the dough into 10-12 pieces.

※ Roll each piece in your palms to make
a dough ball.

★ Take a dough ball and dust it lightly
with flour.

Using a rolling pin, roll the ball into a flat pancake shape. This is your paratha.*

Ask your grown-up to put a non-stick frying pan or griddle onto a low to medium heat on the stove. Granny  uses something called a tawa, which is a very flat pan.

Spray the pan with a little cooking oil. Place the paratha onto the pan and after two minutes ask your grown-up to flip it using a spatula.

After one minute your grown-up should spread some butter on the side that is facing up and flip the paratha again.

* When I make these with my Granny Jas, I roll the dough balls out for Granny while she cooks them one by one.

* Spread some butter on the other side of the paratha.

* Flip the paratha a couple more times to make sure it cooks evenly.

* Slide onto a plate when it is done.

* Serve warm with pickle, yoghurt or curry.

If you like your Indian food spicy, add some green chillies to your paratha dough for an extra kick.

SCIENCE EXPERIMENT!

If you love science like me, Milo and Govi, why not try these fun, easy science experiments you can do at home.

Find out how and why some substances mix and others don't, and discover the amazing effects you can create by adding food dye to oil and water!

1. Make dye drops

Pour some vegetable oil into a tall glass. Add a few drops of food dye and watch what happens.

Food dye

Vegetable oil

> **Each dye drop forms a tight bead shape because dye does not mix with oil, so the drop can't spread out.**

2. Staying in shape

Push the drops of dye gently down into the oil with a spoon and see what happens.

> **The dye drops sink in the oil because food dye is denser than oil. The drops keep their shape because the liquids don't mix.**

3. Exploding dye drops

Fill a tall glass with water, add some vegetable oil and let it settle. Then, add a few drops of food dye and watch what happens.

Oil

Water

Nudge the drops with a spoon to make them sink more quickly.

The drops of food dye remain in a ball as they sink through the oil. When they touch the water, they start mixing with it and form swirling ribbons of colour. The dye continues to mix with the water until the mixture is an even colour.

FOR MORE FUN AND FANTASTIC EXPERIMENTS, CHECK OUT USBORNE'S

365 SCIENCE ACTIVITIES

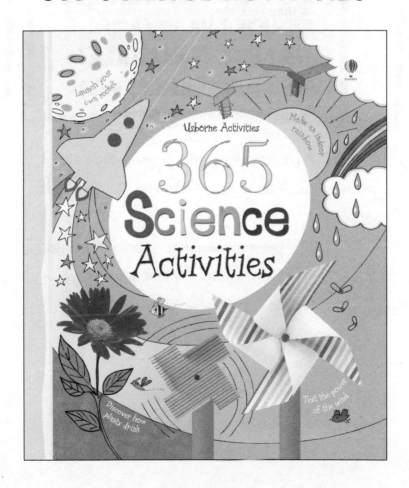

COMING SOON...

Join the Mistrys on their trip to visit the National Space Centre. But it's only a matter of time before Anisha and Milo get wrapped up in some

GRANNY TROUBLE!

Read on for a sneaky peak...

"**ANISHA!** It's time to go! Come on, Dad's outside with the minibus!" Mum shouts from downstairs.

I close my eyes and take a deep breath. Okay, it won't be that bad. Will it? It's just me and my entire family, in a minibus travelling to Leicester and spending four days there. **Together.**

I check my bag one last time; notebook, pen, book on the history of space exploration. One more thing to add. I lean across the bed and pull open the drawer on my bedside table. My silver autograph book. It's one of my most **special** things in the whole world. I flick through the pages. I've got the autographs of the people I most admire in here and this weekend I'm going to add Sangeeta Sanśōdhaka. She is a famous Indian space engineer. When I first read about her it was so **exciting** to see someone who looked like me doing my **dream job**.

And then just last month Milo and I **won** the Schools National Science Fair! The prize was a trip to the National Space Centre. We will get to see actual rockets and space rovers, and by coincidence Sangeeta is going to be there too. She's in England for a conference and is doing some work with the Space Centre so Milo and I get to **meet her**! It's the most **exciting** thing ever to happen to me and I can't wait.

LOOK OUT FOR ANISHA AND MILO'S NEXT RIB-TICKLING ADVENTURE, GRANNY TROUBLE, COMING SOON!

MEET THE AUTHOR

Name: Serena Kumari Patel

Lives with: My brilliant family, Deepak, Alyssa and Reiss

Favourite Subjects: Science and History

Ambitions: To learn to ride a bike (I never learned as a kid).
To keep trying things I'm scared of.
To write lots more books.

Most embarrassing moment:

Singing in Hindi at a talent show and getting most of the words wrong. I hid in the loo after!

MEET THE ILLUSTRATOR

Name: Emma Jane McCann

Lives with: A mysterious Tea Wizard called Granny Goddy, a family of bats in the attic, and far too many spiders. (I promise I'm not a witch).

Favourite thing to draw: Spooky stuff like Dracula's Den in Anisha's first adventure. (Still not a witch, honest).

Ambitions: To master a convincing slow foxtrot.

Most embarrassing moment:

I used to collect old teacups and china. One day, I was in a teashop with a friend and the cup she was using was really pretty. I picked it up to check the maker's mark on the base, forgot it already had tea in it, and spilled the lot all over the both of us. (Witches are too cool to ever do anything like that).

ACKNOWLEDGEMENTS

When I wrote my first book I had a long list of people to thank. A lot of those same people have encouraged and seen me through the writing of this second book in the series. The world has changed greatly since I wrote it but my gratitude for all of their support is greater than ever.

My agent Kate Shaw whose unfaltering support and wise guidance has been such a reassurance during a debut year I could never have expected or planned for.

My editors, Stephanie King and Rebecca Hill, who continue to shape my daft ideas and silly characters into real stories. Without their insight and editing expertise you would not be reading this book.

And everyone else at Usborne HQ who take the pages of my manuscript and send it out into the world as a real thing. My amazement at the process a book goes through and the many hands that carry it through will never cease. Thank you so very much for the part each and every one of you plays.

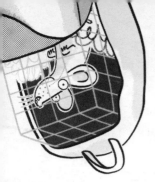

Special thanks to Emma who continues to bring this series to life in the most wonderfully hilarious and vibrant way.

The many authors, booksellers, bloggers, librarians, parents and teachers who have supported Anisha so far, your cheering me on has made being a debut so joyful.

My family and friends, so many of whom keep cheering me on, hand-selling (arm-twisting) copies of the books to unwitting colleagues, friends and acquaintances.

To my precious ones, Deepak, Alyssa and Reiss, my chaos, my calm, my everything.

And last but definitely not least, the readers who have joined me so far on this wonderfully surreal journey. Your reviews, emails and messages really are the absolute best. You guys truly are the ones I write for. Thank you, thank you, thank you.

For more fabulously funny adventures go to:
www.usborne.com/fiction

@Usborne
@usborne_books
facebook.com/usbornepublishing

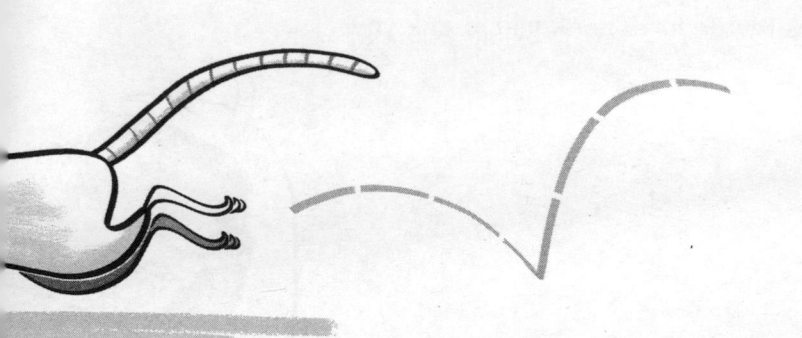